W9-CXV-338

Anna Sun

Dreamers of the Absolute

A Book of Hours

His left hand is beneath my head,
His right embraces me.
Song of Solomon 2:6

A condition of complete simplicity
Costing not less than everything
'Little Gidding,' T. S. Eliot

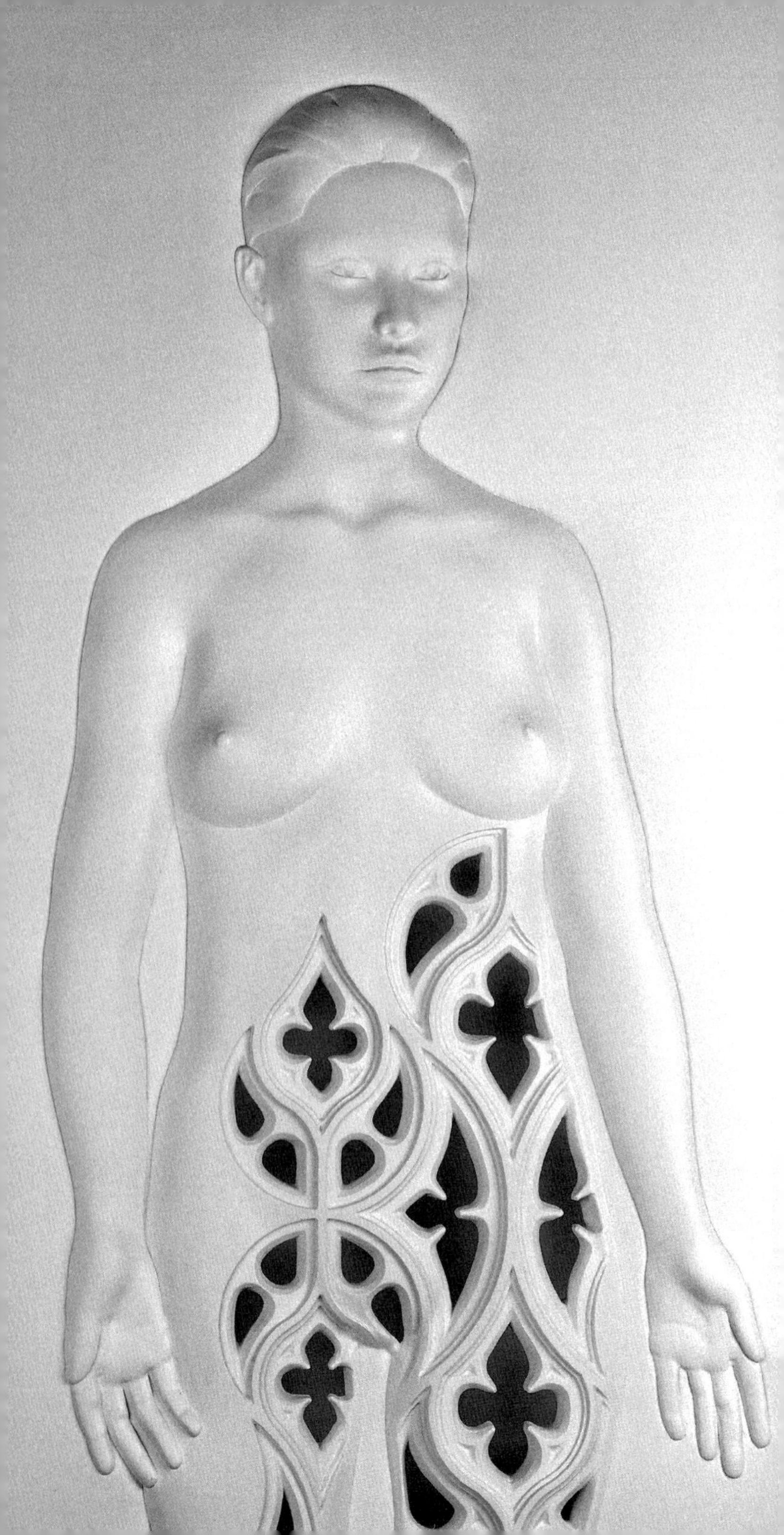

DAY ONE

Midwinter Spring

When Rose arrives at the Abbey, it is already dusk. She is deep in rural Kentucky, a world entirely unfamiliar to her, driving up a small hill that is surrounded by rolling fields and isolated farmhouses, all under a blue, velvety sky. It feels like a dream when she finally sees the white, stately monastery emerging at the end of the narrow dirt road.

She parks her car outside the Abbey gate and steps out. The air is surprisingly refreshing, almost like spring. There is a hint of the sweetness of newly-grown grass, also of the rising evening mist. There is no one in sight, and there is no visible light from the narrow windows that line the fortress-like white-washed walls. The sound of her heels on the stone pavement leaves behind a clear echo.

It has been a long drive from New Jersey, twelve hours in all, and she has spent a night somewhere in Ohio along the way, at the home of a college friend. They had not seen each other since they last danced together to Rose's choreography in their graduation concert. Although she did not want to admit it, it was unnerving to meet her friend's two small children who could already hold a conversation with the adults, and to realize how much could happen in a span of ten years.

Rose is still alone, still unknown in her small professional world, and although not unloved, still unsure of her own heart. And now she is losing her only brother, the only family she is left with after their mother passed away. She is losing him to this grand cloister in front of her, this harsh and imposing structure of angular brick and stone, completely silent in the fading March light.

As Rose looks for the guest-house on the simple map the Abbey has mailed to her, she wonders if this is the right place after all. Or maybe the monks are away on a trip – a pilgrimage, perhaps? The Catholic monastic life is as alien to her as her grandfather's Episcopalian faith, which her mother did not follow, or her father's Asian mysticism, which she has never had a chance to learn to understand.

It is only later that she learns that she has arrived at the time of Compline, the evening prayer. She learns, only later, that as she is stepping into the guest-house, the monastery is just entering into its nightly stillness, the Great Silence.

2

HER KEY HAS BEEN SET OUT for her at the empty front desk in the two-storey guest-house, in a white envelope marked with her name. She has no trouble finding her room on the second floor of the completely silent building. She is relieved to see that, although the room is as bare as she expected, it is also very clean and surprisingly comfortable: a single bed covered with a soft woollen blanket; next to the sturdy desk, a large wooden chair.

She takes off her trench coat and hangs it behind the door, then pushes her small leather satchel under the bed. The satchel is one of very few material objects she inherited from her well-travelled mother, and it has been everywhere with her, since her mother's death.

She walks over to the tall and narrow window to close the curtains. It is not yet dark; she can still make out a small garden under her window, and beyond that, the open field that stretches far into the shadowy distance. She kicks off her shoes, stretches a little, and loosens her hair that has been twisted up into a bun – it has been a long day of driving. It is too late to get dinner anywhere around here, she knows, and she wishes she had brought food with her: some salami, bread and wine.

Only then does she notice two medieval prints of icons on the white walls, also a small cross hanging above her bed. It is a room with a purpose: one is here to pray.

3

SHE SLEEPS WITH THE LIGHT ON, something she always does when she is alone, for as long as she can remember. Yet she still keeps waking throughout the night in the unfamiliar narrow bed, the white cotton sheet getting all twisted under the blanket by her endless tossing and turning. The cell phone she placed by her pillow tells her that it is now almost midnight, and now it is two in the morning . . . She hears birds chirping outside long past midnight, something she has never experienced anywhere else.

She finally falls into a deeper sleep; then she is startled by a prolonged ringing of church bells. She wakes to find that it is still completely dark outside, which only adds to the confusion of her disorientating dreams: What is real, and what is imagined?

In one of her dreams, she finds David in a hospital room. He is sick again, and she goes to see him, not knowing whether he would be happy to see her. As she is walking towards his room, she can see that he already has a woman visitor there, whom he sends away as soon as he sees her. This makes her even more anxious; she almost turns back, but it is already too late. He is asking her to come in.

And when she is standing by his bed, her heart aching because of how pale he looks, he says to her gently: 'Are you here because you are, finally, admitting that you are in love with me?'

4

IN ANOTHER DREAM, she is back to that road trip she took with her brother last May, driving from San Francisco to Big Sur along the California coast in a rented convertible. At the time, she had no idea that Leo was going to enter a monastery in two months. In fact, she thought that he might soon marry his girlfriend Amber, and this trip was perhaps their last chance to travel together as siblings.

Leo did mention that he had made a retreat in a Cistercian abbey at Easter, but she thought it was merely an expression of his new-found interest in Catholicism since his conversion. He converted only a year before, for Amber's sake, who is from a large Catholic family. Although he has never made use of his Masters degree in the history of religion, Leo was always reading theology from all traditions, meditating every morning before going to work in his bakery, something their very secular mother used to tease him about.

Rose was happy to see that Leo was finally grounding himself in a form of faith that was meaningful to him, and it did not matter to her which faith it was. She also thought that he was happy in his new life with Amber. They had been together for five years, since he moved to Boston for graduate school, then stayed on to become a baker. Amber has had a real calming influence on him; Leo is much less intense in her presence, and much more ready to enjoy those small but essential pleasures in life: an afternoon game of pick-up basketball, a late night movie at the Brattle Theatre, a good French dinner cooked by Amber's sister, a rising-star chef.

Amber has been slowly changing the austere interior of Leo's heart, something no other woman was able to do before. Women seemed to be easily drawn to Leo because of his quiet intensity, but they would always leave when they realized the price they had to pay for his fierce concentration. Leo would often disappear into himself for days on end, silently weathering a storm that only he could fathom. For a while he got up at four every morning to read St. Augustine in Latin, and he would live happily on nothing but cheese, bread and coffee, wearing a long-sleeved shirt that had been laundered into a ghost of its former colour and shape. But Amber has stayed, and has brought into Leo's life a quiet joy for the ordinary and the real.

Yet Amber is now left behind, alone and heart-broken. Rose remembers Amber's tear-stricken face the last time she saw her, and turns towards the wall to hide her own tears, also to avert the morning light that is just brightening up the room.

5

IN HER DREAM, she is again standing with her brother on one of those monumental cliffs along the Pacific Coast. The view from the top of the mountain is breathtaking. She cannot see the end of the ocean, for there is no visible distinction between the steel-coloured overcast sky and the immense greyness of the sea. Hundreds of feet below them, the dark-green waves keep crashing into the glistening black rocks, with a rhythm as unrelenting as her own heartbeat.

She begins to shiver when the wind picks up. In her dream, she is only wearing a light summer dress, and the wet, gusty ocean air is chilling her to her bones. Leo wraps her in his arms from behind, his chin resting on top of her head. 'Why are you leaving us?' she asks him, taking holding of his large, warm hands, 'Our love has never been enough for you, has it?'

But even in her dream she does not believe that he would answer her. He is not someone who can easily share his convictions, even though she knows that a stubborn truthfulness is the most essential thing about him. He is truthful to himself and his beliefs, she has gradually realized over the years, and it often means that it is difficult or even painful for others to comprehend his actions. As a result Leo does not like to share his thoughts or emotions, although he always follows them doggedly, the way the migrating geese fly north year after year, even through the most unpropitious storms and lightning.

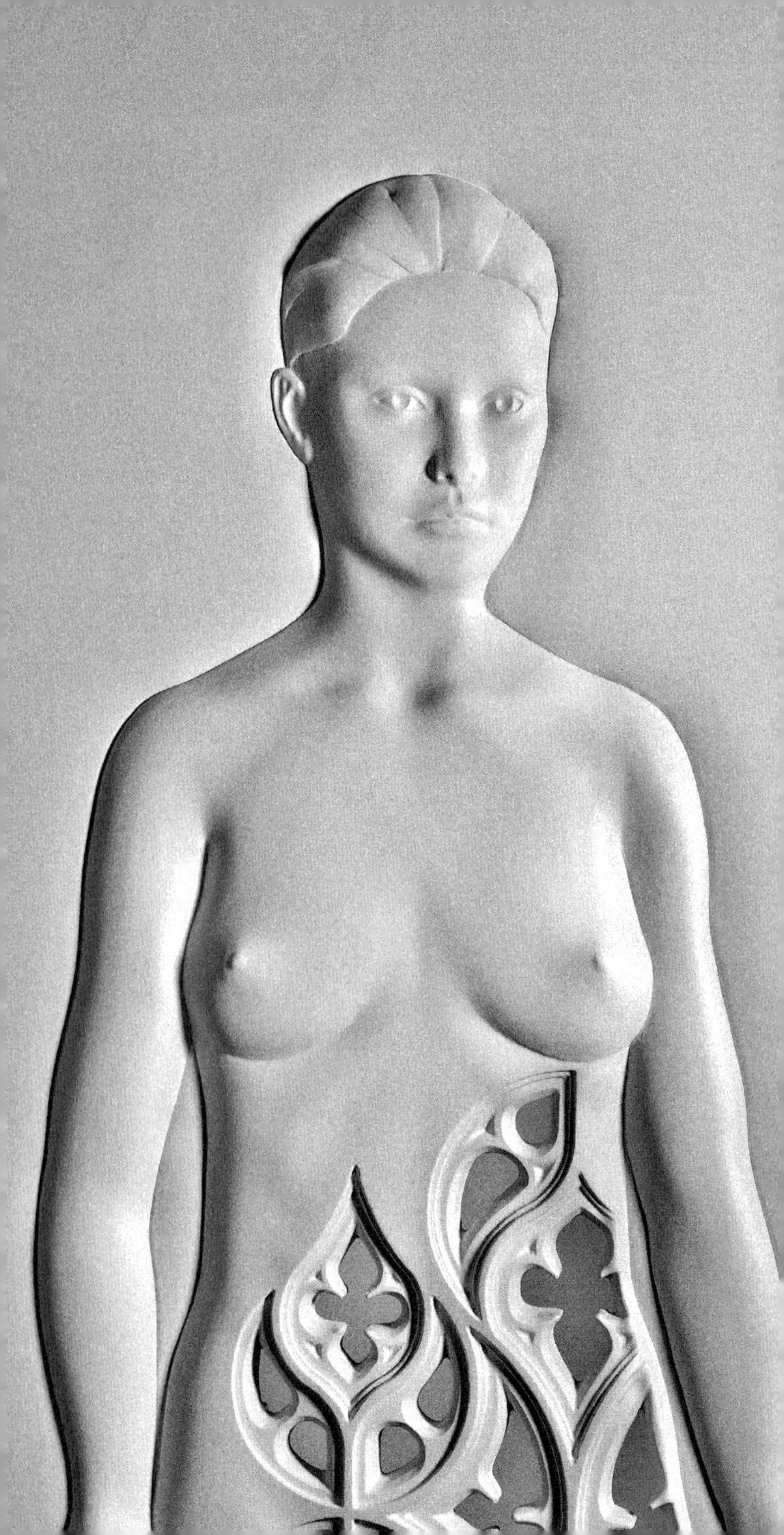

DAY TWO

The Moment of the Rose

When rose finally gets up, showers and dresses, it's already eight in the morning. On her way to the guest dining room for breakfast, she runs into several people in hallways and stairwells, whom she assumes to be lay people on retreat. Yet no one speaks, not even a simple 'Hello' or 'Good Morning'; people merely nod and smile to her. The total silence in the guest-house is astonishing.

'Silence Is Spoken Here,' reads a sign on a table in the sun-drenched dining room. Following other guests, Rose goes into the large and airy kitchen to get food, then sits at a table by a high window with her toast and coffee. There are a dozen or so people around her; the only sound in the room is the clinking of silverware. To her amusement, this conscious silence is not severe at all, but gentle and unforced, like an invisible embrace. She is actually relieved that she doesn't need to socialize with the other guests of the Abbey. What if they ask her why she is here?

And the silence makes her breathe slower, she realizes. Her heart doesn't race as fast, even though she is now more aware of its existence than ever, each heartbeat a step towards something that has long eluded her: a sense of clarity, a sense of peacefulness, the ability to feel without fear.

2

After breakfast, Rose walks over to the front desk to make an inquiry. This time there is someone there: an elderly, frail monk sitting behind the counter, his small frame clothed in a long-sleeved white robe topped by a long black vest. 'Can we talk here?' Rose asks in a whisper, rather nervously. And the monk smiles and nods, his eyes kind and inviting.

Rose explains that her older brother is here in the monastery, that he has been here for six months, and that he has not communicated with anyone in his family for a while. She has written to him quite a few times, but he has responded only once, after having been here for two months, to say that he would stay for good. If he is still here, if it is at all possible, could you please tell Leo that his sister is here to visit him and would like to see him?

It is not as difficult as she dreaded it to be. It does not sound as awful anymore, here in the monastery on a sunny spring morning, when she tells the story to a benevolent monk who must be at least eighty. 'Not to worry,' the monk says cheerfully, 'I will make sure Leo gets the message. Meanwhile, you should relax and enjoy your retreat here. I'm Brother Thomas, and you should feel free to ask for me if you need anything. How is your room? How was your breakfast?'

'Everything is fine, thank you.' Rose is more relaxed now; the hard part is over, and she is suddenly confident that Leo will be happy to learn that she is here. 'I was actually wondering . . . What do monks do all day?'

'Oh, we do lots of different things!' Brother Thomas happily explains. 'We pray seven times a day – what we call choir – and we work as well, making cheese, fudge and other tasty things. When someone is too old, like me, he gets to do the cushier chores, like talking to people at the reception desk.'

'Seven times a day!' Rose is impressed. 'Do you pray together? Are there set times?'

'Yes, sure. We pray in the Abbey church at certain hours every day. You should join us! It is open to anyone who is interested in praying with the monks. The first one is at three fifteen in the morning, called Vigils, which is too early for most people on retreat, but you could probably make it to the second one, Lauds, at five forty-five. Terce, the one we've just finished, is at seven thirty. But you have plenty of time to make it to the next one, Sext, at twelve fifteen, right before lunch.'

'I will try. Thank you, Brother Thomas,' Rose makes an effort to be gracious with his invitation, but the truth is that she is not someone comfortable in religious settings, having grown up with no religious experience at all. Her mother was completely secular; her father sometimes called himself a Daoist, sometimes a Confucian, which were, and still are, mysterious terms to her, for she never had a chance to have a conversation with him about religion, nor going to China with him to learn about what those identities entailed. As a result she has little knowledge of how to behave in religious settings. She was once a dancer in a piece set to a Bach cello sonata in a small church in New York. She left right after the performance, before the evening service, something called Evensong, even though everyone else stayed. Her friend Emma later told her how beautiful it was, how the prayers and the silence flowed together like an endless river.

'Yes, I think you will like choir a lot,' Brother Thomas says. 'Also, you will see Leo there, although you won't be able to talk to him. He will be in the monks' stalls downstairs, and you will be in a separate section for guests on the balcony.'

3

AFTER RETURNING to her room, Rose realizes how much she hates waiting. She has never been good at it; ever since adolescence, she has always been impatient to get to the next item on her to-do list, and this impatience has gotten only worse in the past ten years. She is now driven by the conviction that the more quickly she can check off the mundane task she has to do, the more time she will have for her real life.

There is so much she wants to do, beyond the daily grind of holding a job and paying rent, beyond teaching beginning ballet to college students and slow waltz to newly-weds. All the dances she knows she is capable of making, all the books she still hasn't read, all the films, plays, and concerts she wants to see and hear, all the walks she longs to take on those busy, chaotic, exhilarating city streets, or in deep autumn woods: how can one stand to wait, to live a life bound to a schedule that is not of one's own making?

But now she has to, for there is no way of knowing when Leo will get her message, and there are still three hours until the next prayer – or choir, as the monk puts it. Sitting by the writing desk, with the windows open, she tries to find something to read from the small pile of books she brought with her. There is an old copy of *The Aeneid*; this is a translation David recommended, even though he gave it a mixed review. He was making the case for yet another new translation – his own, which he had been working on for twenty years, ever since the summer he finished his doctoral dissertation on Virgil. She read the epic once before, for a literature course in college, even though she knew too little about the world then to comprehend it. But how much more does she know now?

She picks up the book, and it opens to a page where a small envelope acts as a bookmark. Inside it is a handwritten note on a simple white card, nestled next to a theatre ticket:

> Dear Rose,
>
> It has been a while – sorry that I was out of touch. I did a lot of travelling in the past few months, doing research in Italy and England. I'm happy to be back.
>
> Would you be interested in going to the opera with me during spring break? *Eugene Onegin,* with Karita Mattila and Thomas Hampson. Here is the ticket; hope you will say yes. I have missed you.
>
> David

She still has not made up her mind. She is tempted, once again, to tear up the ticket. But she also remembers what happiness the note brought her when she first received it.

4

WHEN SHE OPENED THE LETTER in the dance studio, the afternoon light was pouring onto the hardwood floor like water. The letter which was sent to her departmental mailbox. She read the note; she put it down, then read it again. Everything around her was quiet, slowed down and suspended in silence, as if in a dream. She watched the pool of light shimmering by the floor-length mirror, with another luminous centre of light rising in its reflection. She was on the verge of joy: he had written to her, after all. Perhaps he had finally understood what was happening to them; perhaps he was finally ready to own up to what had transpired, often wordlessly, between them.

She held the note close to her chest, her fingers caressing his words, as if they were connected to his being.

5

THE FIRST TIME she saw David was in the university chapel. It was not during service, and the chapel, a magnificent nineteenth-century limestone church, was completely empty on that late September afternoon. Or so she thought it was, until she saw him kneeling in a corner.

6

IT WAS ONLY THE SECOND TIME she was in the chapel. The first time was for the opening convocation for the new school year a few weeks before; although the university has long been a secular institution, the chapel is used for formal academic ceremonies. She was surprised by the arrangement, and certainly did not know that she would return here on her own – and so soon.

She came into the chapel with a postcard from Leo in her jacket pocket. The moment she read it in the post office it made her weep. It was terribly embarrassing to be crying in a public place, and she knew she could not manage to walk back to the dance studio, crossing half the campus, with her eyes so red and swollen. The chapel was only a few minutes away from the post office, the only place she could think of that would offer some privacy in such a moment. She ran up to its stately stone entrance, pushing open the heavy wooden doors to seek refuge, to hide herself from the world.

Once she sat down, she took a deep breath of relief. The air in the chapel was unexpectedly cool, with a pleasant smell of wood and leather-bound books. The cold air had the freshness of a deep lake in the heat of summer. She took out Leo's card and read it again:

> Dearest Sis,
>
> You won't believe how extraordinary this place is. I'm in awe of the true ascetic life being lived here. I think I'm going to stay, even though it will be hard for everyone, for a while at least.
>
> Just remember that I love you, that I have been praying for you.
>
> Leo

She was heartbroken the first time she read the card, but now her feelings were different: now she felt anger, mostly, anger at his self-centeredness, anger at his resoluteness. And after the anger dissipated a little, there was also a sense of relief – relief that perhaps, finally, Leo had found what he had been searching for all these years. Perhaps he was finally at peace with himself and the world.

For a while she simply sat there, a few pews away from the altar, trying to imagine what Leo was doing that very moment, a brother who used to take her on motorcycle rides when their mother was again travelling on magazine assignments – the first time was when he was sixteen, and she was only thirteen – and a brother who used to stroke her hair to calm her when she was frightened. And she was easily frightened as a child, whenever there was a thunderstorm and lightning. Her only brother was now a monk praying somewhere in a monastery lost to the world, almost a thousand miles away.

Rose closed her eyes, feeling her face bathed in the faint warmth of the late afternoon sun that was flooding into the chapel through high, painted windows. She tried to pray, which was an unknown act to her, and nothing came to her lips.

7

THE SECOND TIME she saw David was at a crowded reception at the faculty club two weeks later, although she did not know he was going to be there. She normally would not go to such functions, being a mere visiting instructor in the dance program, but Emma, the director of the program whom she had known well since their New York freelance days, invited her to the event and made her promise that she would be there. The reception was to welcome a well-known poet and translator of Homer, followed by a reading of his work.

The faculty club was in a Victorian mansion hidden in an elaborate garden, with paths leading to unknown corners of what Rose imagined to be sites of exotic flowers and trees. When she entered the grand foyer, she spotted Emma right away, talking and laughing with a group of young people in the reception hall, where long tables of flowers, cheese, and fruit were set. Rose decided not to greet Emma yet, but to get a glass of wine instead.

There was a line at the bar. She stood patiently behind two grey-haired professors of Classics who talked animatedly about the latest translation of the *Odyssey*, discussing arcane technical details with evident pleasure. Rose remembered overhearing her art historian father talking in the same way with guests when she was a child, before he moved to California to a new teaching post and a new wife. She always found such conversations rather comforting, like the soothing smell of her father's antique books, or the pungent tobacco scent from his cigar. Her father never hid his disappointment when she became a dancer rather than pursuing an academic career, but she had always known that she wanted to express herself through work that involved both her body and mind.

She walked over to the fireplace in the centre of the room, drawn by the large mirror above it. The intricate gilded leaf motifs on the frame had already faded with age. There was a sheer blue tint to the glass, as if the mirror were a tranquil lake in the afternoon sun, reflecting the transparent blue of the sky. It reminded her of a Victorian mirror she had seen in an antique shop in the West Village. Such lavish items were obviously beyond her means, but she could at least admire them here. As she was trying to look closer, she suddenly caught a glimpse of a familiar face in the mirror.

It was not quite accurate to say it was 'familiar' – she had seen him so briefly in the chapel. But she knew right away that it was him, and she knew it through an inexplicable, deep recognition.

And how different he looked from that day in the chapel! He was now surrounded by people, and he was smiling broadly, nodding approvingly to one, extending his arm to another. There was an air of quiet authority about him; he was no longer lost, nor in desperate need. Then the speaker was introduced to him – she recognized the famed translator's face from the poster for the reading.

'There you are!' Emma's voice was suddenly by Rose's ear. 'I've been looking for you all evening! Are you having a good time?' Emma's warmth was infectious. Rose gave her friend a hug, and they walked over to a corner to discuss their weekend plan: there was a dance concert they both wanted to attend.

But Rose knew that all she was really doing was waiting, waiting for him to come to her. She was quite sure that he had already seen her – the room was thinning; most people had already gone to the lecture hall. But she did not look for him; he had to come to her first, and he had to recognize her in the same way that she had recognized him earlier in the crowd. Emma was still agonizing over whether they should go to the Saturday performance or the Sunday one, since she needed to find a babysitter for her daughter for the evening, when he finally came up to them.

'Here you are,' he said to Rose gently, as if they had known each other for a long time. Then he quickly

turned to Emma, 'You must be Emma? I've heard a lot about you from a colleague of mine.'

Rose did not pay attention to the rest of their conversation: it was ordinary and trivial. But this was what she had anticipated. She knew fully well that a simple greeting was all they could have between them. Yet she could not hide her smile. He had seen her and come to her, after all. Among all the strangers in the room, this one stranger, this man she knew nothing about, brought her an unexpected rush of happiness. He was the man with whom she felt a visceral, almost sacred, bond. She saw the same eyes that she had seen in the chapel, although now there was an easy smile on the face that she remembered from that lonely hour.

But that face in the chapel, lined with ruefulness and sorrow, was already forever engraved in her mind.

8

THIS DESIRE . . . how should she describe it? They met for drinks a week after the reception; they simply ran into each other on campus, and walked together a few blocks to his favourite cigar shop, which was a place she walked past often, but had never ventured into.

Unbeknown to her, it had a book-lined back room lounge with a few faded dark-red leather armchairs. The soft yellow light of the Tiffany lamps made the late afternoon hour feel like late night; the Scotch he ordered for her – he urged her to try it – only deepened this sense of illuminated darkness. She did not mind the cigar smoke in the air; her father was a smoker for many years, until the last two years of his life when he was dying of cancer. The smell of strong tobacco actually brought her a faint sense of comfort, as if her father had just left the room.

Then she saw David on a commuter train going to New York the day after their afternoon together, standing next to a tall young woman on the platform. She noticed the woman first because of her striking platinum blond hair, cut extremely short. Rose was only a few steps behind them as they were all getting onto the train, and she noticed his right hand gently pressing the woman's slender waist as they were entering the crowded carriage. Sitting as far away from them as possible, Rose made sure that he would not see her. She was not hurt, but she knew clearly from then on that she needed to proceed with caution. She needs to be careful with her heart.

Two weeks after that, they ran into each other once more on the street in the early evening, and she took him to her favourite neighbourhood bistro just around the corner. They talked for hours, longer than the first time; when they were standing on the sidewalk outside the restaurant to say goodbye with a rather formal handshake, the street was already deserted. It must have rained earlier: there were wet yellow leaves all over the pavement, gleaming in the golden light from the shop windows all around them.

She saw him again in December, in her dance studio, something she both tries to remember and to forget. And the last time she saw him was in early January, during winter break; there was already heavy snow on the ground.

9

THEY COULD EASILY HAVE BECOME LOVERS, but they both avoided it, encircling it, wary of its consequences. What did they want from each other? What did they have that they could offer each other?

The first time they met for drinks in the cigar lounge, when her hand brushed against his by accident early in their conversation, a wave of intense warmth radiated from that briefest of touches, charging the air with a tangible tension, a delicious, unacknowledged bond of desire. When she lifted her heavy Scotch glass, she could sense the bond being stretched by the tiniest movements of her arm, as if there were an invisible elastic string between them. She could break free from it only by moving far, far away from this man sitting next to her, his elbows resting on his knees, his head lowered, his breathing deep. She felt the flow of heat spreading through her body like a low-grade fever when they resumed talking after a brief, delicate pause, in which both of them fell momentarily silent.

Through it all her mind was following the discreet course of desire that had entered her body, how it was moving from her hand to her arm, from her shoulder to her chest. It was like a ray of sunshine lighting up the pale façades on an empty street, building by building, in the earliest hours of dawn.

10

BUT HOW DOES SHE EXPLAIN this desire, when she holds the memory of him in the palms of her hands, caressing each remembered moment with such tenderness?

The change of seasons: from autumn to winter, only three weeks. On the first weekend of November, the leaves were still lavish, all jewel-toned red, gold and brown, like tapestries made of velvet threads. She listened to old French chansons on her drive home. What sensuous joy to be accompanied with Cora Vaucaire's silken voice singing *Les feuilles mortes* on her way back to her small apartment every evening, the sky a dark and transparent blue, the leaves rolling onto the windshield like drunken birds, their rich feathers catching the last rays of the setting sun.

Then, two days before Thanksgiving, the snow-storm came, and the leaves were all gone overnight. Facing the white, frozen ground through the three large windows in the dance studio, she felt there was something momentous in this simple passing of seasons, something grave and cruel in this austere transformation. She suddenly realized how real he was, an actual person beholden to time and change, but her desire was weightless, a mere shadow of real emotions that she knew he deserved. She was almost ashamed of herself, for her solipsistic indulgence in these obsolete melodies of longing.

II

ROSE GOES TO THE ABBEY CHURCH for the first time at noon, for the prayer of Sext. She walks up to the balcony of the church through a long corridor that connects the guest-house with the main monastery building, a short cut whispered to her – in order not to break the rule of silence – by a middle-aged man on retreat she has just met in the guest-house. They briefly introduced themselves; she learned that he is a psychiatrist who has been making frequent visits to the Abbey for ten years.

She could hardly wait for the divine office to start. She has come all this way to see her brother, and she no longer cares that she has to see him like this for now. Just a glimpse of Leo's face will make her happy, just a chance to wave to him to let him know of her presence, just a meeting of their eyes to let him know that she still loves him, no matter what life he has chosen to live.

When Rose sits down in the second pew on the balcony and takes in her surroundings, she is awed by the church's overwhelming austerity. The space is startlingly spare, with no adornments that she can discern. The ceiling is at least 30 feet high, with the walls painted alabaster white, the rough textures and the irregular lines of the bricks still visible. Daylight has clearly distinguished the narrow high windows from the walls, showing the muted colours and patterns of the painted glass, which are surprisingly abstract, considering that the church is at least 150 years old.

Yet there are also refined, exquisite touches everywhere, giving the church an ascetic elegance: discreet, white speakers fastened to the walls, smooth wooden benches with the lightest layer of blonde paint, a lone flowering tree – with several red blossoms – near the extremely bare high altar, with nothing but a simple wooden cross. She has learned from a history of the monastery that the church was completely renovated

50 years ago, transformed from a traditional church into this radically stark, almost brutalist style.

How well the changes have served the space, she thinks: there is nothing merely ornamental in this light-filled place. Everything serves a purpose; the clarity is breathtaking.

But she is also getting anxious about seeing Leo in this magnificent, impersonal setting. Will she be able to recognize him in the choir stalls, from this balcony high above him? She tries to hold on to her memory of the physicality of him: his broad swimmer's shoulders; his endearingly awkward gait. Has he shaven off his thick hair? She started cutting his hair when she was in middle school; their mother had a haircut kit for boys, and Rose took over the haircutting duty the day they all realized that their mother was never going to be patient enough to pay attention to the evenness of his hairline.

She liked the monthly ritual of draping a black nylon cape around Leo's shoulders in the middle of their small kitchen, giving him a simple crew cut by using the clippers that came with the kit. That was before he went to college, and she still cut his hair now and then when he visited her in the years that followed. She always tried to make a nicely tapered neckline by carefully shaping the hair around his neck, making sure that the line behind his ears was clean. She was a rather fussy barber, and Leo was always good humoured in enduring her exacting sessions, his strong, bony neck bent forward under the light pressure of her hand.

He was a man of strength even then, and this was something she understood without being able to articulate it. There was quiet vigour even in his partaking of daily chores like this; she often had the sense that he was made for something magnificent and distant, and he was gentle with her only because he knew he would leave her some day, and he wanted to be loving with his little sister before he had to take on the true weight of his power.

12

THE HANDFUL OF RETREATANTS on the balcony suddenly rise. She stands with them, following their every movement, anxious to do everything right in order not to stand out as an outsider. Now she sees that they have risen to pay respect to the monks who are entering the church. There they are, about thirty of them, in floor-length white robes and long, black hooded vests, filing into the space below them unhurriedly, each quietly taking up his seat in the choir stalls, which are three long rows of seats with very high backs, all made of pale wood.

She sees Leo right away, the only young man among elderly monks. She knows it is Leo, yet she cannot quite recognize the brother she has known all her life. Dressed in a long white robe without the black vest, with his hair cut extremely short, Leo has a different presence from before: there is no lightness of step, nor looseness of posture. He moves with a precision she has never before seen in him, and when he stands, there is a rigour that surprises the dancer in her. He seems so strong and calm; his appearance is almost majestic. She is not getting emotional at all in seeing Leo, as she feared; she is overwhelmed, so unexpectedly, by his transformation.

Yet when the prayers begin, her heart tightens all of a sudden. She watches him bowing slowly with the other monks to mark the beginning of the divine office; it is a deep bow of reverence and devotion, expressed with a heartfelt tenderness. And it pains her so much to see it, for she recognizes instinctively, not as a sister but as a woman, that it is an expression of total submission and surrender. This is submission from someone who has never before submitted himself to anything in his life; this is surrender from someone who has not before yielded himself to anyone, even though he has tried so hard to fall in love.

Tears slowly fill her eyes, blurring her vision of Leo in his white prentice monk's robe. She realizes that her brother has finally found the great love he has been searching for, the kind of love to which he could – and will – give his life.

DAY THREE
Shirt of Flame

This is Rose's third day in the Abbey. She has set the alarm on her cell phone to three in the morning, but she is awake even before that. Like the night before, there are strange birds singing long past midnight, and she keeps waking to their voices. It is both disorienting and enchanting, as if she were staying in a realm of mysterious timelessness.

After seeing Leo yesterday, she has made herself a promise that, from now on, she would follow all seven divine offices during her time here, so she would be living the same life as Leo. The first prayer, Vigils, is an imperative.

When the church bell rings at three fifteen to signal the first divine office of the day, she has already been up for a while, having stretched, showered, and finished her first cup of coffee. It is not as difficult as she imagined, starting the day at this pre-dawn hour. On her way to the Abbey church through the silent, well-lit white corridors, she feels a lightness in her step, a sensation of anticipation and hope.

2

When she enters the Abbey church, it is still pitch black outside. Only the lights in the centre of the church are turned on, illuminating the high, empty space right above the monks' choir stalls. Sitting in the semi-darkness on the balcony, Rose is glad she has wrapped a large wool shawl around her shoulders, for the unheated chapel is much colder than her room. It makes her remember that it is still March, a time caught between winter and spring.

The thirty or so monks are now entering their stalls one by one, each bowing unhurriedly towards the direction of the high altar that is hidden in the darkness, before settling down in their seats. She sees Leo right away, sitting in the same seat as yesterday in his white novice's robe, one of the tallest men in the choir, his head lowered in a gesture of prayer that is now already familiar to her. After quietly shuffling their prayer books and adjusting their robes, the monks are finally ready for Vigils to start.

A few more minutes of silence pass. Then from the centre of the choir comes the clear, sharp sound of a tap: the Abbot has just signalled the start of the divine office by hitting a small piece of wood on the high back of his own wooden choir stall. Then everyone stands and waits, until a monk breaks the audible silence with a simple prayer in a clear, low voice:

> O Lord, open my lips.
> And my mouth shall declare your praise.

After a brief moment of silence, a monk walks up to the small podium at the end of the choir section and speaks into a small microphone, reading the first psalm of Vigils. On the high balcony where Rose sits, the monk's voice is heard through a discreetly-placed sound system, and the psalm seems to be spoken by someone standing right in front of her in semi-darkness, with barely concealed need and urgency:

> When I fear, I will trust in you,
> In God, whose word I praise.
> In God I trust, I shall not fear:
> What can mortal man do to me?

After he finishes the reading and returns unhurriedly to his seat, the light suddenly goes out completely in the chapel, imposing a darkness that is as astonishing and potent as the silence that ensues.

A few minutes later, a flicker of light comes back to life on the small podium, illuminating the prayer book while the next elderly monk takes his place there and quietly chants the next psalm. The small patch of light reveals part of the weary face of the monk who is reading, also his short white hair and his black scapular, his white sleeves dimly visible in the dark:

> O God, make haste to my rescue,
> Lord, come to my aid!
> As for me, wretched and poor,
> Come to me, O God.
> You are my rescuer, my help,
> O Lord, do not delay.

3

ROSE GOES TO THE GUEST-HOUSE kitchen right after Vigils. It is almost four in the morning, and there is another prayer, Lauds, coming up at five forty-five. She has decided not to return to her room, since she knows she'd be tempted to go back to sleep if she is near her bed at this hour. She wants to keep vigil between the morning prayers; she imagines that Leo is reading in his cell at this very moment, and she wants to follow faithfully the rhythm of his life.

There are already three or four people in the brightly-lit kitchen getting coffee and breakfast. The robust aroma of strong coffee and fresh toast makes Rose happy. She nods her morning greetings, and people smile warmly back, there is an unspoken camaraderie in their shared commitment to these early morning prayers, which most retreatants do not bother with.

By now Rose has seen all of them, even though they have not exchanged a word. There is a young woman in her early twenties, always in a college sweatshirt. Is she still a student? There is a young man in his thirties in a long black robe, yet she cannot tell whether he is also a monk, for his robe and belt look quite different from what the monks here wear. A third person is a young man in secular clothes – a buttoned-down black shirt with black slacks – yet she has noticed that he has been attending the divine offices in the monks' stalls. Who are they? How long have they been here? Why are they here?

While she is getting her second cup of coffee, she notices a monk standing next to her, waiting for his turn. He must be in his sixties, and he smiles warmly when he meets her gaze, as if he were inviting a conversation. She feels unusually energized this morning, fuelled by caffeine and the rigour of the routine of divine offices; as a result she speaks to him light-heartedly and impulsively:

'How do you do it? How do you keep the passion alive?'

As soon as she says it, she senses how dramatic she must have sounded, and she regrets right away this misguided informality. To her surprise, the monk laughs and answers in the same playful tone:

'The secret is that we are not high most of the time! You have to do choir seven times a day, every day of the year, not missing any as long as you are a monk. The key is not to expect too much, not to think too much, just be in the moment for the prayers, and be as open as you can.'

The monk then introduces himself: Father Bernard, the master of the guest-house. This is the reason why he is mingling with the retreatants and getting coffee in their kitchen; the other monks are cloistered in the monastic side of the Abbey, with little interaction with the guests.

Rose wants to talk to him some more, so he signals her to follow him from the kitchen to the other end of the dining room. She notices for the first time the small room next to the entrance of the dining hall, a special space designated for talking: this is where people go when they wish to have conversations during their silent retreat, either with other guests or with a monk.

4

THE WINDOWLESS yet comfortable room is decorated with a few simple chairs, side tables, and tall table lamps. Once they sit down, Rose surprises herself by asking about Leo first; she does it without thinking, but Leo is really what has been on her mind ever since she arrived here. Father Bernard answers unguardedly, telling her that he already knows she is Leo's sister.

'Leo has chosen to take a rigorous vow of silence before he formally becomes a novice, which is the first step towards becoming a permanent member of the monastic community, so it's quite unfortunate that you are visiting him now,' Father Bernard says, looking sympathetically at Rose, his gentle face framed by receding grey hair. She can tell that he is getting tired after Vigils: his eyelids are heavy, and he takes long pauses throughout their quiet conversation. But when he does respond to her questions, he answers thoughtfully and reflectively, as if every word Rose utters is of equal importance.

Father Bernard's white habit and black scapular make him look like a priest consoling a parishioner, but Rose cannot be consoled so easily, for she does not understand the faith upon which Leo is now building his life. Yet she is beginning to be in awe of the monks' actions: this intensity of action in the seven daily prayers, this strict observance of silence. And she asks Father Bernard about the meaning of such a life, about what it is like to be a monk here for forty years, even though she knows she does not have the right to speak so freely.

'Have you ever heard of the "dark night of the soul"?' he asks, and he smiles kindly when she shakes her head. 'But you certainly understand it: it is the moment of doubt of one's faith, when one questions the value and soundness of one's commitment. What if everything we do is in vain? What if God is not going to answer us directly? We have to affirm and renew our faith constantly, out of necessity. This is why we are so focused on our prayers and contemplation, no matter how long we have been here. We ask ourselves over and over again, every single day: How close can we get to God? What should we do in order to live in

God's grace? What should we do in order to get closer to the ultimate truth? Don't you ask these questions as well, Rose?'

5

ROSE'S CONVERSATION with Father Bernard has a forthrightness that is strangely familiar to her. After attending Lauds, the next divine office, at five forty-five, she goes back to her room to read, and it dawns on her then where the familiarity comes from: her conversations with David, which always amaze her with their utter directness.

But this is something quite rare for her; she is known amongst her friends for her reticence. Her reserve does not come from an introverted temperament, which is what people tend to assume, but from her deep-seated distrust in having oneself understood by others in any truly meaningful way. Leo is one of very few people who could get behind her façade. Until – she now realizes – David appeared in her life.

6

'ROSE, DO YOU REMEMBER that writer, that famous one, who was visiting here earlier this year? I know several women who are still desperately in love with him. How about you? Did you find him irresistible as well?'

David was stretching his legs out elegantly in his leather armchair, sipping Scotch as he spoke. Their corner of the cigar lounge, where they met back in October, was again enveloped in a comforting evening glow. She was sitting in a chair next to his, with a glass of single malt in hand, yet she was not in the same relaxed mode at all. Her back was not touching the curved back of her chair; her dancer's posture was awoken by a sudden passion rising up in her spine.

'I never wanted him, if that's what you meant. He is brilliant, he seems to be capable of strong emotions. He writes about his love for his wife in the most natural and touching way. But I've never desired him . . . Of course, he is incredibly attractive. I was seated next to him at a dinner once, and he was witty, sharp, and unfailingly gracious. But he does not need me or any other woman; he already has someone he loves who has made him whole.'

'But after all, isn't it desire that you are after, Rose? To desire and to be desired?'

'But that is never enough, is it? I want to be desired and needed, in the most profound way: you need me in order to complete who you truly are.'

7

'I HAVE BEEN REREADING the *Aeneid*. Fame, power: is it really so central to a man's life?' Rose asked when they had fallen deeper into their conversation, where they felt comfortable to think out loud, as if speaking to oneself.

'As you know, the *Aeneid* actually did not bring fame or power to Virgil. Virgil asked his friends to burn the manuscript before his death, but the emperor Augustus overruled his last wish and gave the poem to Varius and Tucca to cut and modify in order to publish it. That's how we still have the *Aeneid*.'

'Have you been after power in your own life?'

'I came to success rather late. My first book on Virgil and empire was very severely reviewed by people in my field. My second book fared only slightly better. But I knew it did not matter; the ones who did not get my books were the ones on their way out. What I desperately need to do now is to finish this book on Virgil and T. S. Eliot, and there are at least three other books that I want to write. But how much time do I still have left? Virgil died when he was 51 – I will be 51 next year. You speak as if you know my life, but you are younger and more hopeful; you are looking at a different horizon.'

'But perhaps something else matters more. Didn't you mention that the death of Virgil and the birth of the historical Jesus were within a single generation?'

'Indeed. Aeneas, the brave son of Venus, was soon replaced by the saviour of human sufferings, the son of God. People started to follow Jesus barely 50 years after Virgil's death. The last line of the *Aeneid* reads: '*vitaque cum gemitu fugit indignata sub umbras*.'

David paused for a second before translating it: 'With a groan and indignation, his spirit fled under the shadows.'

WHEN THEY RAN INTO EACH OTHER for the second time on the street, she invited him for an impromptu dinner at her favourite corner bistro. Throughout the evening he implored her to say more about her being 'a fundamentalist of the emotions,' a term she told him a friend had invented to label her.

'But how do you know whether these powerful emotions of love or passion you speak of are real, Rose? Couldn't it be that they are merely what you want to feel? A few years ago I was seeing a married woman, and she said she was madly in love, wanting to be with me no matter the cost. She indeed had a lot to give up. But the trouble was that I didn't know if I was truly in love with her. We have all known manufactured emotions, feelings we think we ought to have. In the end, how can you tell the difference between a genuine longing and an artificial one?'

'This is the only thing I'm sure of – I'd be nothing without it . . . ' She knew she must have sounded incredibly naïve, but she had to say what she believed to be true: 'I do not believe one can fake a powerful emotion. One cannot pretend to be deeply moved.'

She wanted to say more about the remarkable clarity of passion – those strong emotional, sensuous attachments, so visceral in nature, a yearning in one's chest and belly for the touch, voice, and smell of the person one loves, a tangible need impossible to be dismissed. This is why throughout history there have been lovers who give up everything simply for the sake of being in the arms of the beloved, without whom one's own life would be empty, pale, not worth living.

But she was stopped by David's smile, a smile that was more wistful than ironical, as if he wished he were wrong.

9

THAT NIGHT ROSE REMEMBERED her favourite scene in *War and Peace*. When the young Natasha first falls in love with Prince Andrei, she is an impressionable teenager who would soon be seduced by a strong physical passion she feels for another man. When she declares her love for Prince Andrei, he responds with great gentleness: 'You do not yet know yourself.'

Sitting across from David in this small restaurant, talking and laughing as the night grew deeper around them, she had enough self-knowledge to know that she was already a different person from the time of her first love. She told David that now she knew where her desires might lead her, what she could and could not endure, what prices she was willing to pay for love.

David looked at her almost tenderly: 'But, Rose, perhaps there are prices you are not even aware of.'

10

'OH, HAVEN'T YOU HEARD about David Morton's divorce?' Emma said to her when they met for lunch a few weeks after her dinner with David. 'His wife left him several years ago for a friend of his, and you can imagine how it caused quite a stir at the time!

Too bad I don't know the details. But I did hear that he was crushed by it. My friend in Classics told me that he almost drowned swimming up in Maine in the summer after his divorce. There was a rumour that he probably wanted to die, since he went swimming in a lake all by himself on a cold foggy night.'

Their waiter had been trying to get their attention, and now they had to turn their minds back to the lunch table, which was piled with empty sushi plates, with edamame shells scattered everywhere, like fallen green leaves after a storm. There were hardly any other customers left in the restaurant, so they had to get ready to leave. Emma helped Rose, strengthening the wide collars of her men's trench coat, something Rose took from her father's closet a few years before his death. 'Oh, I forgot to mention that last year Morton had major surgery – a bypass, actually,' Emma said. 'Too young for someone his age, of course.'

Rose kissed her good friend good-bye, and they walked out into the bright afternoon together, the cold early winter air pleasantly caressing their flushed cheeks. But Rose's mind had already returned to David. She had a sudden urge to see him again; she had a sudden urge to place her hand on his chest, right above his scarred heart.

II

IT IS ONLY NOW, sitting in this small room – her monastic cell – in a white abbey in the rural South, so far away from her own world, that Rose finally understands what she really meant back then, towards the end of that luminous autumn night, when she leaned forward towards him to speak of how desire would not be enough.

Because the beloved deserves it; because anything less is not worthy of him, and anything less is not worthy of her own heart.

12

AFTER TERCE AT SEVEN THIRTY, the last divine office in the morning, she goes back to her room and collapses into a dreamless sleep. She manages to get out of bed to attend Sext at twelve fifteen, then a silent lunch, followed by the office of None at two fifteen. She admires the solemnity of the prayers, but this intense schedule is already beginning to take its toll. She feels utterly exhausted when she finally returns to her room in the early afternoon.

There are three hours until the next prayer, Vespers, which starts at five thirty. She has not yet heard back from Leo; she has queried one more time at the reception desk before lunch, and was told by Brother Thomas that she'd have to be patient in waiting for his response. Leo has not lifted his eyes even once to search for her on the balcony during the divine offices since her arrival. Although it does comfort her to see Leo in the church, he seems to be moving further and further away from her, even in her presence.

She lies down on the thinly carpeted floor. This is how she relaxes: not on the bed, but on the floor, any floor. It grounds her, and she trusts the immediate connection she has with the floor, the foundation for movements throughout her life as a dancer. This is her anchor in the open, thin air in which dance takes its shape – a space that is as dangerously formless as the sea.

She wonders what David is doing this very moment. She knows that he is still in New York. Is he alone? Is he thinking of her? A warm wave of desire suddenly overtakes her body, overwhelms her. She closes her eyes.

13

ROSE WAS RESTING in the middle of the dance floor after teaching her class when David walked in. It was in early December, shortly after the first snow storm. The sun was setting fast; she had just turned off all the lights, and the west-facing studio was bathed in the dark pink glow of the faraway tides of evening clouds.

This was her favourite time of the day. She would often lie there for half an hour after a long day of teaching, sometimes imagining new movements in her head, sometimes simply relaxing her back and legs, letting the smooth, cold hardwood floor take away the stress of dancing. Today she was looking forward to a long stretch of quiet relaxation; Emma was in a committee meeting, and she was coming back to fetch Rose for their weekly dinner around the corner in about an hour. Still in her dance clothes – a faded black leotard and a soft, loose pair of grey yoga pants – Rose stretched out her legs, and took a deep breath.

She heard the soft opening and closing of the heavy door, then two or three clear footsteps. She lifted and turned her head slightly to the left side of the studio to see who was coming in, half-expecting a student who had forgotten a sweater or a book, for she knew Emma must still be in her committee meeting.

But it was David standing by the door, looking quite ill at ease in his silvery navy raincoat in the darkening studio, smiling at her uncertainly. This was the first time she saw him looking awkward in any way or form, a man of the world being thrown into her bare, open space, a stage contained by three walls of windows, with the fading sun reflected in the floor-length mirror. But it was endearing to see him fumble in her presence, like an ordinary suitor; a rush of happiness filled her heart.

She smiled at him and lowered her head back to the floor. She could hear the racing of her heart, she knew she could not speak, and she knew she could not trust her voice. There was suddenly a wave of heat rising in her throat, and her lips were burning from this surging fever. She tried to breathe deeply, to get rid of her increasing light-headedness.

She closed her eyes, but she could still feel him standing there – his presence was no longer a merely visual one, but physical as well: he had changed the consistency and weight of the air in the room. She could now feel him on her fingertips and her arms, on her chest and her stomach – the presence of him was enveloping her entire body. She took several deep breaths, and a stream of warmth suddenly flowed from her face all the way down to her thighs.

A minute or two must have passed when she opened her eyes and turned to him again. He was still standing there, although he had put his leather satchel down. Now he no longer looked uncomfortable or self-conscious; he was in control again, and he was watching her, touching her with his eyes. She felt weak and helpless, and he took it all in, silently acknowledging the power she had handed to him.

He walked over to her, slowly and assuredly, but this time she could no longer hear his footsteps. Her senses were heightened and altered in unexpected ways; all she could hear and see and feel was the diminishing distance between them, and each of his steps stirred in her waves of luscious sensations. Did he feel the same? She wondered in her silent delirium; did he know that he was wading through the river of her desire, and every one of his steps was changing the shape of the water?

He took off his coat, and sat down next to her. He did not touch her. She could smell his aftershave, a faint old-fashioned scent of tobacco and nameless wild flowers. She could also feel the warmth radiated from his body, so near and so strangely familiar to her, his chest under his smooth black wool jacket and slightly rumpled white shirt. She wanted to sit up and be embraced by him, but in her weakness all she could manage was to lift her left arm and close her eyes again.

She felt her hand being held in mid-air, and his hand was not at all what she imagined. He did not have the long, delicate fingers that his elegant demeanour suggested: his hand was large and almost rough, and his palm was much warmer than her own. But it did not matter how cold her own hand was, for as soon as his hand touched hers, an immense heat spread through her body, and she lifted her head and chest involuntarily, as if electrocuted by his touch. She could now hear his breathing getting closer and faster; before she could comprehend what was happening, she felt his left arm lifting her up, and suddenly she was sitting on the floor facing him, her breasts pressed against his torso. As if in a dream, now his warm lips were on hers, a dream that took place in a balmy, open, bottomless ocean, with waves holding them up, embracing them in their embrace.

During their long kiss, which seemed to last forever, his left hand continued to firmly hold her, supporting her neck and the back of her head, a gesture of both strength and tenderness.

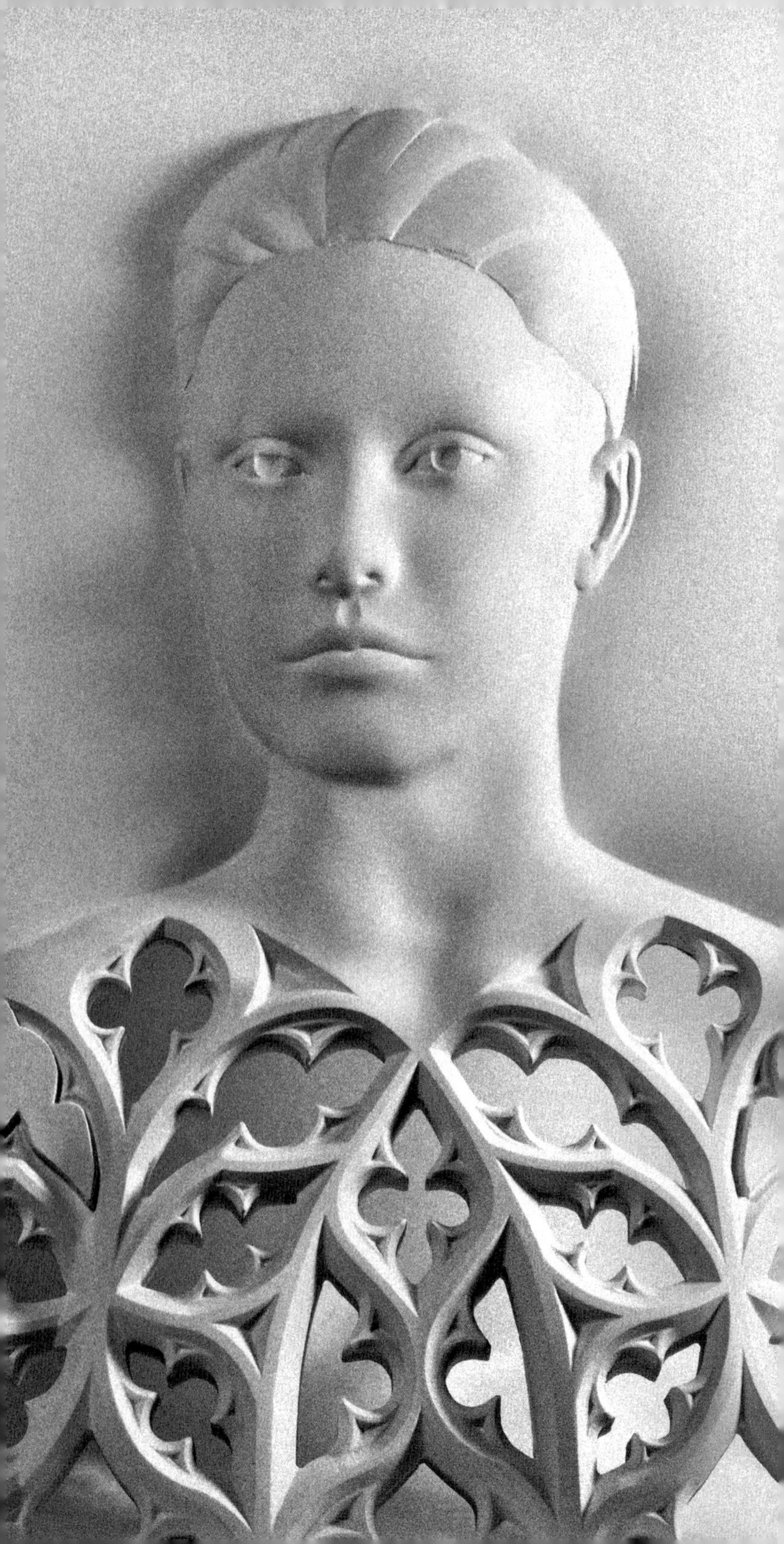

DAY FOUR

While the Light Fails

ROSE REMEMBERS once seeing a young woman sitting in an airport lounge, alone and crying. She cried as if she had lost everything that ever mattered to her; each sob came with a shudder, and she caved her shoulders in to protect herself from the violence of her grief. She was miserable, inconsolable, and oblivious to the rest of the world. It was clear to anyone watching that she was suffering from love.

Rose wishes that she could walk over to this woman now to ask why there can be no solution for her unhappiness. She wants to gently talk to her and help her dry her tears. She wants this young woman to share what it feels like to be so desperately in love, but she also knows that there is no way of knowing what this love is without being the one with the aching heart.

She knows this because she is looking at a vision of herself from her own past. She has been saved from the fate of drowning in the dark depth of sorrow, yet that love she used to know in the hollow of her chest, that love that she once cried every night for and was willing to die for – she fears that it is now forever lost to her.

2

SO MANY THINGS TO SAY, yet so little time to say them . . .

She knows that the window for articulating what one really feels and needs is closing. She will only stay in the Abbey for three more days, and she has to find a way to fully accept the fact that Leo is not going to return to her world.

For years she has been trying to anchor her emotions by listening to certain pieces of music or rereading certain novels or poems. She always has her music player with her whenever she travels, and she cannot bear taking the hour-and-half train ride from New Jersey to New York without listening to those familiar pieces of music that have been with her throughout her adult life – love songs of Leonard Cohen, Joni Mitchell, and Bob Dylan, flamenco, tango, old French chanson, the occasional opera aria or piano sonata.

And there are books everywhere in her apartment. She reads in bed, at her kitchen table, on the sofa in the living room at night. She always has at least one novel she is reading with her; sometimes there are two or three on her night-stand, so she could move from one imagined life to another when she feels restless.

And she often takes a book with her when she takes a bath in her large, old-fashioned tub, for she cannot stand the emptiness of that isolated moment. There is a quiet noise of void that she can hear when she is in the bath alone, or when she is in bed by herself, which she can easily chase away with stories of love and loss, happiness and sorrow. This is something she has learned to do since she was fourteen, when her mother started to fall slowly apart after the death of Leo's father, a married man she loved from afar for too many years, seeing him whenever he could steal a few days away from his wife and large family, which meant weeks or months of longing on the part of Rose's mother, seen and eventually pitied by her children.

But now she has no access to her music or books; now, in the total silence of the Abbey, in this place where every single day is devoted to the search for absolute clarity, she has to learn to listen truly to her own heart.

3

TO LIVE DEEPLY. This is her only wish. Not to live happily, but to live deeply and truthfully. It is not happiness that one is after in love, it is the purity and clarity of one's heart.

4

THE LAST TIME Rose saw David was in January, in the middle of winter break, before he suddenly disappeared from her life.

'I thought it was you whom I saw in the library lobby earlier today,' he said to her almost shyly, standing by the door of her small reading carrel in the library. 'Am I interrupting?'

'Not at all!' She closed her book and stood up, not quite knowing how to respond to his sudden appearance. She had been reading a collection of early-twentieth-century Russian dance criticism, preparing for a dance history class she was about to teach next term. How did he manage to find her in her carrel deeply hidden in this enormous library? But instead of asking him, she simply said: 'Shall we take a walk?'

The sun was shining brightly through the glass roof covering the long corridor, which circled a great part of the library. There was thick snow everywhere outside, weighing heavily on roofs of buildings. But her heart felt buoyant, as if it were already spring. Walking by her side, he kept buttoning and unbuttoning his black wool jacket, one that might have been sharply tailored some years ago, but now had lost both its dark shade and its thick texture, which in turn had added an unexpected melancholic elegance. For some reason this put a smile on her face.

'What were you reading just now?' he asked, and she told him about her task. 'Oh, do you mean you are studying the history of dance?' She nodded, and they walked in contented silence for a few seconds before turning a corner. She stopped in front of a huge pair of windows, which faced a quiet courtyard, where a few shiny, bare branches of birch were bathed in afternoon sun.

'I know you have been to Paris . . . Have you seen the tapestries in Musée Cluny?' he asked, and she nodded again. She had only been to Paris once, as a college student. She was more interested in vintage clothing and dance clubs back then, even though she did dutifully go to all the art museums, so she could report back to her father.

He smiled: 'There is a story about Balanchine that I like, a story I'm sure you know well. He once took the young Suzanne Farrell – when she was perhaps twenty – to Musée Cluny when the City Ballet was performing in Paris. He took her to see the *Lady and the Unicorn* tapestries, and he stopped in front of the final one, '*À mon seul désir*', trying to tell her that she was his heart's desire. But she was very young, and distrusted his love because he was still married. You must know the rest of the story better than I do – how they lost each other in the end.'

She certainly knew the story well. In fact, she had read Farrell's own account of the visit to the tapestries in her autobiography, how Balanchine told her that he wanted to make a dance for her about the unicorn and the virgin in the tapestries, which became the three-act dance *Jewels*. But David's version was much more wistful, as if he were the heartbroken one in the story, as if he were the lover who had tried – and failed – to tell something true to his own unattainable beloved.

They did not speak for what seemed to be a long time. It might have only been a minute or two, but it was a long and comfortable silence, and she felt closer to him in that moment than ever. Her body was conscious of his presence, yet he did not awaken in her the kind of inflaming desire she experienced in the dance studio. It was an unspoken tenderness that was enveloping her, slowly seizing her heart.

She put her right hand on the window. The glass had been heated by the sun all afternoon, sending a pool of warmth through her open palm.

5

TO BE DEEPLY MOVED by someone, a moment of being profoundly touched – isn't there an imperative to be true to these experiences? To be true to the moment when a new desire seizes one's entire being.

She remembers their kiss in the dance studio more vividly with every passing day: the exhilaration of the first intimate contact with someone, the dizziness of the realization that, this man, who was now in her arms for the first time, was as much a sensual being as herself.

Sitting in her room, still an hour to Sext, the last morning prayer before lunch, she has an overwhelming desire to see David again. More than anything, she wants to hold him, to caress his eyes, his forehead, his hair; she wants to feel his actual existence with her fingers, through her touch, once again.

6

THE ANCIENT STORY of Dido the tragic queen. She kills herself when her lover Aeneas leaves her to fulfil his destiny as the founder of Rome. When Rose was 18 years old and had to study *The Aeneid* in a literature course in college, she felt a chill running down her spine when she read Dido's lament, for this was what she saw her own mother go through during her long affair with her married lover, Leo's father.

He was a reserved, serious man, always dressed in a well-tailored suit when he came to their little house to pick up Leo for a rare afternoon outing. He had never had a real conversation with Rose, but he was always wonderfully courteous with her even when she was little, making her feel important and grown-up. And when Rose was in her early teens, she began to guess that he was still seeing her mother, for her mother would disappear for a long weekend once in a while, and would bring back gifts to Leo from him. She was often emotionally volatile after such weekends, sometimes elated and full of laughter, sometimes irritable or tearful. Rose did not understand that he was never married to their mother until the year of his death, when Leo blurted out that he could go to the hospital to see him, but not their mother.

When he died, their mother was crushed by grief, a grief she could not share with anyone outside their lonely home. Rose later realized, as she was reading about Dido, that her mother might have killed herself the way Dido did. The only reason she did not do it was because she had two children that anchored her to the world.

But her mother started drinking heavily after the death of the love of her life, something that changed her character forever. She was never again the same witty, joyful person that Rose and her brother knew, which is why Rose and Leo became so close in their teenage years. Together they had to survive their mother's drunken rage and her tears, and to find a way to make sense of their lives all on their own.

Dido's suicide is magnificent in the *Aeneid*, despite how well the Romans understood the horror and repulsiveness of death. Art often makes such tragedy seem thrilling, yet Rose learned early on in her life that a powerful love can destroy and ravage; there was nothing magnificent in her mother's heartbreak and sorrow.

She puts down the book and forces herself to name the entangled emotions in her anxious heart. There is desire when she thinks of David, yes, and the longing for its fulfilment; there is pleasure also, the joy of recognition, the elation of finding someone who shares one's own vision of the world. There is anticipation as well, the sweet delight in seeing one's own unspoken yearning echoed in another's gentle response.

But most of all, there is fear: the fear for the overwhelming force of need, when one surrenders oneself to another; the fear that she would be in that bottomless darkness again, looking in vain for an unconditional love that could anchor her, a love she feels is forever beyond her reach. She has already had her fearless venture into the wilderness of passionate love, and escaped its flame with her sanity barely intact; she no longer has any illusion of its transformative power.

Yet she is also aching to be in that place again, to feel that high, flaming wind caressing her face, once again.

7

SHE REMEMBERED TELLING DAVID last autumn, at their dinner together, that she was reading a new biography of Edith Wharton. It was written by a brilliant British biographer, a woman, she added.

'Why do you think it makes a difference that it's written by a woman?' He asked in earnest. Now she can explain to him why it mattered.

It is a well-documented story that in 1907, when Wharton was forty-five, she fell passionately in love for the first time. It was her first true love after years of bitter disappointments in her marriage and she gave herself without reservation to her lover. For him – a refined but withdrawing seducer who had a complex emotional and sexual life – it was merely another amusing love affair.

For her, the first year of their affair was full of stolen meetings and 'blissful hours', but over time he grew distant, often unresponsive to her pleading letters. When they resumed their affair after a brief separation, the biographer wrote:

> But everything was different: she had lost confidence.

The loss of confidence when a woman loves without being loved back: only another woman can articulate it so perfectly, Rose thinks. Only a woman can capture such heartbreak in so few words.

8

IN ONE OF WHARTON'S many letters to her lover, she spoke with astonishing truthfulness and gentleness:

> Dear, there was never a moment, from the very first, when I did not foresee such a thought on your part as the one we talked of today; there was never a moment, even where we were nearest, that I did not feel it was latent in your mind. And still I took what you gave me, & was glad, & was not afraid.
>
> You are as free as you were before we ever met. If you ever doubted this, doubt it no more.

Rose remembers the letter well. But could she say the same when the time comes? Could she be unafraid?

9

IS SHE GOING to New York to see him? The opera is merely a pretext for something more: a dinner afterwards, a night spent together.

She realizes that she cannot allow herself not to make a commitment about visiting him if she keeps speaking to him in her mind like this. She has to be true to these feelings and expressions of longing, for the expressions themselves are not enough. She feels the urge to honour such expressions with concrete actions; she cannot speak of love without living it.

What she longs for is precisely the actual, the real: his body, his mind, his heart, here in her arms. To love is to be faithful to one's heart no matter the cost. And to love is to be there with the beloved until the very end, facing the unavoidable illness, misfortune, pain, and loss.

So to love is also to fear, fearing the moment in which the beloved no longer loves one back, or the moment when the beloved ceases to be in the world. Like the way her mother was destroyed by the death of the man she loved, years after he abandoned her to return to his family.

And yet anything less is a shameful trivialization of love, she knows; anything less becomes a mere cynical game of the heart.

10

HE WHISPERED TO HER that evening, before they parted:

'I want nothing less than everything from you.'

11

SITTING IN HER COLD ROOM after Vespers, as the day grows darker, she is conscious again of the fact that now, especially now, she is completely alone in the world. She has been an orphan since her father died two years ago; in the short span of five years, she has lost both of her parents. It seems melodramatic to think of herself in such terms, for she is of course a mature adult, living independently, no longer forging her identity as the 'child of', and was in fact not particularly close to either of her parents before they passed away.

But she is now truly alone in the world, a free-floating vessel on a vast ocean, with no island in sight. There is no familial face she can turn to when she needs undivided attention; there is no longer anyone with whom she can have a fierce fight – the kind she used to have with her mother when she was in her teens and twenties – without having to worry about its consequences. There is no one with whom she could just be, without having to justify her actions, her intentions, her worth in the world.

And she has also been released of her obligation to love: she is now free not to love at all. The love and affection amongst friends is a choice, not a duty; she is now freed from any compulsion to live her life with the need of others in mind, for there is no longer anyone expecting her love, not even her presence at a particular Thanksgiving or birthday dinner, even though she often complained about such insistences in the past. There is no longer anyone who needs her, whose happiness depends on her care and love.

And there is also no longer anyone whose love for her she can take for granted, she realizes, now that Leo is disappearing from this world.

12

SHE SUDDENLY FEARS that she is drowning.

She was never a good swimmer. She is usually fine when she swims in a pool, a controlled environment where she can always return to the shallow end if she loses strength or confidence. She likes knowing that absolute safety is within her reach, only a few feet away at the end of the blue tiled pool, marked 5'4, and that she could always manage to return there, and be able to stand with her head above water, her feet firmly touching ground, taking a deep breath.

But now there is no safe harbour in sight. Now she is alone at sea; there is no firm ground for her to stand on. The ocean is bottomless and merciless, and the shore is far, far away. She feels a slight panic rising in her spine, even though she is merely sitting quietly on the edge of her bed, a book open in her hands. It is getting darker outside with every passing minute; the night is going to be as bottomless as the ocean.

She is wary of this sinking feeling, a prelude of dark nights of anxieties and fears to come. She asks herself whether she needs to seek help. She has had very limited experience with therapists; for a few months after her father's death she saw a psychiatrist weekly, until she came to the conclusion that he was not telling her anything she did not already know. He prescribed an anti-anxiety drug for her, which she carried in her purse for an entire year, yet she did not take it, not even once. But it was consoling to know that the pills were within reach, that the promised safety and clarity of mind was within reach.

It is vaguely comforting to know that there is a psychiatrist right here in the Abbey, a fellow retreatant. She had a rather nice conversation with him yesterday after dinner, when they were both taking a walk in the garden outside the guest-house, where silence doesn't need to be observed. She learned that he has been coming here for a few days every month for ten years, treating monks who need psychotherapeutic help in the monastic enclosure. He did not give her any details, but he did speak of how much he admired the kind of life the monks lead here – 'heroic,' he said. He also told her how vulnerable one might feel when one gives oneself away completely to God, who may or may not respond. And how psychologically dangerous it is, he remarked, when one loves and surrenders without reservation, with one's full heart.

13

THE ONLY WAY to save herself is to keep swimming, she knows, yet she fears that she may not be able to stay afloat, for it is always, for her, an act of confidence rather than capability.

And her confidence has everything to do with the nearness of solid ground, of the immediate presence of safety and shield.

14

ROSE SAYS TO DAVID in the chapel, during Compline, the last prayer of the day, as if in a dream: 'I'm on the verge of true love . . . Should I take a step back? Do you wish me to take a step back, staying on safer ground, safe from the absolute demands of the heart?'

And she hears his voice whispering by her ear: 'Darling Rose, yes, take a step back . . . How can we know if we will be able to catch each other if we fall too deeply? Be safe for me, for I do love you.'

15

ALL OF A SUDDEN, she feels how fragile her body is, all breakable bones and soft flesh. And the world around her is made of nothing but hard substances: concrete, rock, iron, steel and stone. They could crush her so easily, now, overwhelm her with their hardness, with their utter indifference to her anxieties. It feels like a miracle that she could have survived in the world for so long, living her life without the recurrences of such tantalizing fear.

16

THE SKY IS A DARK SHADE of blue when she leaves the Abbey church after Compline. Instead of walking back to the guest-house through the inner corridor that connects the buildings, she takes the side exit and walks around the church through the graveyard, where generations of monks have been buried on the same gentle slope.

There are no ostentatious gravestones, only simple wooden white crosses planted closely next to one another, each no higher than her own palm, marking the graves with nothing more than the names of the monks and the years of their birth and death. She has walked through this grassy slope during the day, and now the rows of white crosses are barely visible in the dusk, faintly reflecting the light from the Abbey church, like faraway stars seen on a night sea.

Rose is usually uncomfortable with graves, but this cemetery tonight feels close to her heart. She has seen a brief footage of a Cistercian burial: the body of the deceased monk, dressed in his white habit and wrapped in a grey blanket, was slowly lowered into the grave by fellow monks. A monk was standing in the grave to receive the body, holding it gently before lowering it to the ground. There is no coffin for the Cistercians; they are to be covered by nothing but soil.

Seeing that one-minute footage brought tears to Rose's eyes. She had known the finality of death from the passing of her parents, but she was now understanding for the first time how one should accept it as part of the unrelenting cycle of life. It felt true to the words of Ash Wednesday, something she has learned from Leo: 'Remember that thou art dust and to dust thou shalt return.'

The white walls of the Abbey now look almost blue in the growing dusk. Looking towards the guest-house, she can see the brightly-lit dining room through its large windows; there are people moving about, getting ready for the Great Silence. In the stillness that surrounds her, the sudden ringing of the bells ripples through her entire body, as if she were made of water. These colours, movements, and sounds, also the freshness of the evening air and the gentleness of the grass under her feet, give her an unexpected rush of happiness. They offer her a deep sense of peace and relief, which feels, now, like love.

DAY FIVE
The Moment of the Yew Tree

THERE IS LIGHTNING throughout Vigils this morning, the fifth day of Rose's stay in the Abbey.

The lightning is silent yet bright, illuminating the windows and dark corners of the church at unexpected intervals. A storm is rising, and will be upon them soon, but the church is as still as ever, a ship held together by nothing but prayers offered at dawn. It has withheld the most turbulent storms for a hundred years, and it will continue sailing on through the immense darkness all around them, saved by the love and devotion in these prayers.

Rose notices a monk kneeling by his seat before the divine office starts. Monks often stand next to their seats facing the high altar for a few minutes before sitting down in the stalls to meditate, a common way of expressing reverence. But she has not seen anyone kneeling before prayers until now.

Such a simple gesture, so early in the morning – and so deep at night – breaks her heart. There is both fragility and strength in the monk's gesture: both fear and love, renunciation and surrender.

2

AFTER A BREAKFAST of warm oatmeal and strong coffee, in the silence she is now used to, Rose returns to her room.

She patiently sifts through the scattered items on her desk, and the deep silence pervades everywhere: in the church after the Eucharist, where a few monks stay on to meditate on their own after the formal prayers; in the kitchen and the hallway, where greetings are exchanged with silent nods. This deep silence has given her clarity of mind that she did not know existed.

What she is sorting through on her desk seems to represent the perpetual messiness of her life. There is the letter from David, for instance, with the opera ticket peeking out from the envelope. There is her notebook, which has dance notations, clippings, drawings, and all sorts of other notes related to the dances she is working on, although she has not touched the notebook since her arrival here. There is Emma's postcard from Seville, where she is attending a flamenco workshop, something they had dreamed about doing together. There is also a black-and-white photo of Leo, Rose, and their mother sitting in an outdoor café somewhere in Greenwich Village, their arms wrapped around one another, taken a year before the car accident that took away her mother forever.

There are a few books as well: *The Rule of Saint Benedict*, *The Cloud of Unknowing, The Aeneid*, and *Four Quartets*. She realizes that she is now reading them in order to understand the people she has loved.

3

SHE IS ALMOST LATE for the divine office of Terce at seven-thirty. She is startled to see that it is about to begin in three minutes when she wakes from her thoughts. She runs up the stairs to the Abbey church, and almost bumps into a monk on the landing, who is coming out of a door in the corridor that connects the Abbey church with the living quarters of the monks. She has never seen anyone use this door before; this monk must be running late as well.

She hastily says 'Hello,' before realizing that she is not observing the rule of silence. The monk is a little startled too, both by her sudden appearance on the stairs and her greeting. He acknowledges her with his eyes without responding, and hurries down the stairs to enter the church through the entrance reserved for monks.

Only after she sits down does a sudden recognition come to her. She realizes that this is the monk who was kneeling by his seat this morning at Vigils, before prayers started. He is perhaps only in his thirties, and not unlike Leo in his age, carriage, and devotion. Before she knows it, her eyes are already filled with tears, and a sharp pain washes over her like a wave.

4

THE NEXT OFFICE, Sext, starts at twelve fifteen, which lasts for only fifteen minutes. Then it is time for lunch, technically called 'dinner' in the Abbey, the most important meal of the day. Everyone stands quietly in line to get the same pasta dish, made with fresh mushroom, a meal both simple and refined.

After lunch, Rose carries her plate and coffee cup back into the kitchen, and thanks the two middle-aged women in white kitchen uniform for the delicious lunch. They tell her, to her surprise, that their job is merely setting up the meals and cleaning the kitchen;

the meals are not cooked by them, but by the monks themselves. In fact, even the dishes are brought back to the monastic enclosure to be cleaned.

How could she have been so careless about using one coffee cup after another! This genuine humility of the monks – cooking and cleaning after praying for her – overwhelms her. She has been reading *The Rule of Saint Benedict* during her lunches, rules of monastic life given by Saint Benedict 1,500 years ago, and she realizes that they are still being followed strictly in this abbey: seven divine offices daily; no speaking unless necessary; requisite manual labour that supports the abbey; aversion to everyday comfort; simplicity in clothing, serenity in movements, and reverence in all conducts. She has not seen a life so committed, so focused, and so selfless before.

A phrase from an old poem comes to mind, something she has read a long time ago: ‘Life justified.’

5

SHE WALKS BACK to her room after lunch, her own breathing the only sound discernible in the long, carpeted corridor.

The day is going to be nice again, perhaps even warmer than yesterday. There is not a single cloud in the high, clear sky outside her window.

6

THE PRAYER OF NONE starts at two-fifteen, lasting only twenty minutes. The next prayer, Vespers, won't start until five. The end of None marks the beginning of the afternoon of manual labour for the monks.

Leo knows Rose is here, yet he has not looked up at the balcony searching for her, not even once, since her arrival. She is his only family left in the world, yet he has not once tried to meet her gaze. He has the clarity of heart to stay true to who he is here in the monastery, and trusting that she will be able to comprehend his actions, and not stop loving him out of anger or doubt.

7

ROSE SITS THROUGH None with a faint fatigue, for it has indeed been tiring for her to get up at three every morning, something her body is not used to. She feels a kinship with the retreatants who have persevered in attending all the daily offices; it is almost as if they were all part of a secret society, bonded by their shared belief in rigour.

She notices again the young woman with long, curly brown hair in her early twenties, who sits not far from her. They had a hushed conversation early this morning, on their way to the kitchen after Vigils. Maria is from San Antonio, Texas, with bright eyes and a funky sense of fashion, more like a college student into Björk than someone discerning a monastic life. But here she is, focused in her search for a life of prayers.

And then there is Peter, a man in his late 30s from Northern Kentucky. He has a warm smile and Rose had a chance to talk to him yesterday outside the Abbey church. Peter is a contractor who has built many houses in his hometown, where he is part of a large Catholic family and who had once been engaged to be married. But he constantly feels that he is called to a life of religious devotion, he said, and this is why he is seriously considering becoming a monk. In fact, he has already donated his property to charities, and he has tried out one other monastery already, a Cathusian order in Vermont. He found the rules there to be too strict; the silence is absolute, unlike in this abbey, where communication among people is still possible. This is why he is asked to join the monks in the choir stalls for the prayers while still taking his meals with the retreatants and living in the guest-house. He is weary of studying Latin, even though the ability to read Latin is no longer a necessary part of monastic life.

Rose has talked to Father Bernard about the tensions and conflicts in a monk's life: the crisis of faith, the constant threat of tedium, the danger of taking daily offices as mere formality. Yet none of the darkness Father Bernard mentioned can be detected in him; there is a quiet glow of trust and generosity in Father Bernard, as if coming from a luminous centre deep in his being. She has the feeling that Peter will be able to live the same form of life.

8

NOW IT IS TIME FOR VESPERS, at five-thirty in the afternoon.

The prayers begin as usual: a psalm, then a doxology sung slowly, each word pronounced with clarity:

> The God who is, who was, and is to come,
> at the end of the ages.

Nothing is hurried in these lines, even though the words are sung dozens of times every day. The utterance of 'the ages' ends on a slightly higher note, like a hopeful plea.

There is something deeply moving in it, even though the monks are only singing a simple phrase to praise God, even though it is not in the dark hours of Vigils, but in the gentle, transparent light of an early spring afternoon.

9

AFTER VESPERS, a few monks stay in their seats to meditate, and a few retreatants on the balcony stay on as well. Rose sits there until the last monk leaves, then goes back to the guest-house to get coffee.

Brother Thomas calls after Rose as she walks past the reception desk. 'Rose, would you like to meet with the Abbot?' he asks. 'I just spoke to him, and he said that he would be glad to talk to you, since Leo cannot see you this time.'

Rose had a few chats with Brother Thomas already, and had once called him the 'sage monk,' to which he replied, with a mischievous smile: 'But sage is only a herb!'

Their conversations often go like this:

'How do you get clarity?' Rose asks.

'You come here, and you realize: it doesn't work. Nothing works. This is how you get clarity.'

'But monastic life does work, doesn't it?'

'It works because it doesn't work. This is the gift of grace. The ones who have breakdowns are the rational ones; only rational people go crazy.'

'What is the Abbot like?' Rose asks now, a bit nervous because of the unexpected invitation to speak to the head of the monastery.

'Oh, Father Jerome is a very nice man! You will enjoy talking to him,' Brother Thomas smiles. 'He is very serious and very intense – he is a real theologian, with all the degrees you can get! And he is a good young man, with a big heart. But I don't know yet if it will work out for the monastery. He is very strict about following the Rule, stricter than most previous abbots, which is great, but not everyone is happy about it. And he is too thin! The next time I see him I will tell him to eat more.'

'But you are very thin as well,' Rose reminds him.

'Yes, but I'm old and I have small bones, you see, and I am not an abbot taking care of forty troubled souls.'

10

ROSE IS SUPPOSED TO MEET with the Abbot in the small visiting room next to the dining hall, where she had her first conversation with Father Bernard, but she is early for her appointment and finds the room empty.

She wanders out of the glass door of the dining hall that leads to the garden outside, where a few small pink and yellow flowers are bathed in warm afternoon light, the first spring blossoms she has seen this year. There is a tall monk standing there, with his back to her, talking to a worker who is repairing a mowing machine. Behind them is the open valley below, a vast field of light green rolling hills, with a few farm houses in the far distance, their white roofs glistening in the sun.

She watches the monk intently. He is standing perfectly erect and she notices how the lower half of his loose white robe flaps gently in the breeze, a stark contrast with the solidness of his posture. There is a stillness in him that sets him apart from the worker he is speaking to. He seems to carry within himself a silent solemnity, a quiet yet defiant break from the world. She knows this must be Father Jerome, even though she has only seen him from a distance before, during prayers in the Abbey church.

Having finished his brief discussion with the worker, which ended with a hearty laugh from both men, he turns around and sees her. 'You must be Rose?' he asks her with an open, easy smile as he walks over to her. Standing quite close to him now, Rose sees that he is only in his late forties, and he seems even younger than his actual age, with his shaved head, thin-rimmed glasses, and dark, kind eyes. He certainly looks bookish in his black and white robe, yet the brisk way he walks to the visiting room with her and the overall ease with which he carries his tall body makes him seem almost athletic.

11

FATHER JEROME SITS facing Rose in the small visiting room, not shifting his attention away from her for a single second during their conversation. Rose is grateful for his attentiveness, and she likes his mild manners and easy laugh. But what strikes her is the sense of moral seriousness in him, an effortless gravitas that sets him apart from all the other monks she has met. He has a quiet yet profound form of charisma; she can easily imagine treating him as a moral superior, which is essentially the job description of an abbot in a monastery: St Benedict spoke of an abbot as someone who is entrusted with caring for the souls of the monks in his charge.

The first thing the Abbot says is how sorry he is that Leo cannot see her during her visit. Leo is in the middle of a silent retreat, he explains, and Leo has explicitly instructed that he should not be disturbed by anything or anyone.

'So does this mean that he might not know I'm here?' Rose asks with sudden hope. The Abbot nods his head, as if expecting this question: 'Leo did know that you will be here, right before he decided to start the silent retreat, and it is clear that he has chosen not to pursue any communication with his family, at least for now.'

After saying this, he sighs almost imperceptibly, and takes out a small bundle from a hidden side pocket of his slightly crumpled robe. Rose sees at once that these are letters, all unopened, and she recognizes a few of her own blue envelopes. It is quite possible that the rest are all from Amber, since they are the only two people who know about Leo's new life. 'Leo asked me a week ago, before your arrival, to give you back these letters, and he said that he trusted that you would return them to their rightful owners. May I entrust them with you?' The Abbot stands from his seat as he is saying this, and it is obvious that her audience with him is over.

Rose takes the small pile of letters, held together by an old rubber band, and is surprised by how light they are – yet there is so much love, so much pain, and so many tears in them. So this is the sum of the life Leo has left behind, and he has decided to have nothing to do with it. Rose knows Leo has never been a sentimentalist, but she is suddenly angered by the fundamental melodramatic gesture of his returning of these letters, and the selfishness of such a resolute sign of renunciation.

The Abbot is about to take his leave, extending his bony hand to Rose. She stands up as well, and before she realizes what she is doing, she says in a shaky voice she can barely control, for she is already on the verge of tears: 'Is this how monks live their lives? Just leave people who love them behind, leave all passions and responsibilities behind?'

The Abbot does not seem embarrassed at all by her outburst. He simply stands there, his hands again folded behind his back, quietly considering her question while Rose weeps, clumsily using the sleeves of her white shirt to wipe her tears. When she finally looks up at him, he speaks kindly and clearly, making sure that Rose is hearing his every word:

'I'm glad you are staying with us, and I hope you will stay for more than a few days, so you can get a sense of the rhythm of life in the Abbey. I cannot explain our life to you unless you can discover its essence for yourself. But there is one thing that I hope you will understand some day: this is perhaps one of the most passionate lives a person could choose to live. Now, if you would excuse me . . . It has been a real pleasure meeting you.'

12

AFTER THE MEETING with the Abbot, Rose cannot bring herself to attend Compline. She has been sitting in the library, pretending to read while trying to collect herself, shaking from both heartbreak and embarrassment. When the bells ring for Compline, she suddenly realizes that what she really needs to do is to get away from here, to get some fresh air from her own, non-monastic world. She is not yet ready to leave the Abbey completely, but she needs to spend at least one evening away. There is a small town only half an hour from here, and she remembers driving past a few restaurants when she was on her way to the Abbey, which now seems to be such a long time ago.

She gets up from her chair, a little unsteadily, and walks out of the library. She walks past the white Abbey church, then the guest-house. She feels disoriented, as if in a confusing dream from which she

wishes to be awakened. She is now walking past the iron gate that leads to the monks' garden, inscribed with the words 'God Alone.'

On her first day here she almost went into the garden by mistake, pushing open the unlocked gate to try to get a glimpse of the stone pond and the winding paths leading into the woods behind the Abbey. But of course she is not allowed into it; the garden is part of the monastic enclosure, the world of Leo's for the rest of his life, a world that is forever closed to her.

13

THE DRIVE to the nearby town is unexpectedly soothing, with open fields and meticulously groomed horse farms passing her in the growing dusk, as if in a beautiful silent film. She stops at the first restaurant she sees on the edge of the town square, and finds it an old-fashioned tavern with a dark-wood bar, still empty at this early hour.

She asks for a strong drink, and with a warm, encouraging smile the waitress points to a list of local bourbons on the menu. Rose has never had bourbon before; she orders a shot of Woodford Reserve at the recommendation of the waitress. It is intensely flavourful, infused with the smokiness of burning wood and flaming fire, even stronger than the single malt Scotch that David has taught her to drink.

But she finds it difficult to bear any sound in the tavern, not even the subdued chats between the waitress and the bartender. She changes her seat in order not to face the flashing screen of the television at the bar. When two other early diners arrive and choose the table next to hers, their light-hearted banter with the waitress makes her wish she were sitting in complete isolation.

14

THE LONGER SHE IS IN THE TAVERN, the more she misses the monastic time she has grown so used to. She keeps thinking, throughout her solitary meal: now are the last prayers for Compline; now it's time for the Abbot's benediction. Later, after her glass of bourbon is taken away: now, the Great Silence.

After what seems to be an interminable time of endurance, during which she tries to adjust her breathing, centring herself so as not to be bothered by the sounds around her which are sounds of real, joyous, ordinary life, she realizes what she needs is absolute silence. She needs a silence that is total and uncompromising, where she can close her eyes and be true to the most important things in her life. And with each passing minute in the tavern, there is an increasing hollowness in her heart, an almost tangible emptiness.

And this is an aching need that she now finally recognizes: this is the same kind of hollowness left in her heart when David disappeared from her life earlier this spring, after their ineffable closeness. It feels like a parting from something that is essential to her, something to which she has given herself without knowing.

DAY SIX

Between Two Waves of the Sea

THE BELL FOR VIGILS startles Rose. She hurriedly puts on a large black wool sweater over a long-sleeved shirt, for the limestone Abbey church is always colder than her room. The sweater used to belong to Leo – he left it in her apartment several years ago during one of his unannounced visits. On this chilly morning, this is the only thing that makes her feel that he is still part of her life.

It is time for prayers again, and she learns one of the most basic things about prayer: it comes from necessity, not choice.

2

QUIET CHANTING AT VIGILS. She can hear in the monks' voices both their weariness and their hard-earned serenity. And her brother's voice is indistinguishable from others, impossible to be known again.

The lights do not go out during the prayers. She learned yesterday that the momentary darkness she so loved is reserved only for special days of the week. But the lights are turned off after the prayers are over, after all the monks have gone back to their cells. The church is now completely still, as tranquil as the clear, cold night outside, a white ship floating soundlessly in a calm, moonlit sea.

3

THERE WAS ONE MOMENT, only once, when she saw David's soul laid bare. He lifted his eyes up to her in the darkening university chapel when she walked past him on that late September afternoon; it was as if his entire soul was exposed in that glance.

She felt an irrational urge to respond. There was a sorrow in his eyes that moved her beyond reason; he was in mourning, and he shared it with her, without any pretence, by accident as well as by necessity. He must have intuited that she was someone who could understand it, and she did, taking in his mourning as if it were her own.

When he looked up from where he was kneeling, they were the only two people in that silent, secluded place. He must have seen her sitting in the far right corner, her face in her hands. He must have already known her when he greeted her wordlessly as she was taking her leave; he must have already recognized the familiar emotional forces that governed her inner life.

There was an extraordinary sense of recognition when she took in his face – and, as she lately realized, his soul. She did not even notice whether he was old or young. She simply recognized the eyes of a man who was facing his despairs and hopes alone, in silent prayer, and she was suddenly overwhelmed by a sense of communion, an unconditional feeling of love that bonded her to him, as if they were lovers sharing a most intimate moment of tenderness.

4

IN HER DREAM a few nights ago, David was resting in a hospital bed, ashen and weak, when he asked her: 'Are you here because you are finally admitting to yourself that you are in love with me?'

She cannot remember what she said to him in the dream. The rest of the dream was lost to the cold, dark night, but she does remember that lingering taste of sweetness under her tongue when she woke, like the memory of a long ago happiness, a faint assurance of a joy that she has now forgotten.

If he were saying the same thing to her now, talking to her as she is standing by the window in the pale March sunshine with her coffee, shivering slightly from the early morning chill, she knows how she would respond: 'Do you remember what Tatyana says to Onegin? She says to him, both in the garden when she first declares her love for him, and later, in her married home, when she tells him that she can no longer be his: 'I love you – why dissemble?''

5

THERE IS A SELF-PORTRAIT by Lucian Freud, painted when he was already in his 80s, which Rose saw in real life and now sees in her mind's eye. In the portrait, the painter is standing naked in an empty, harshly-lit room, with a painter's knife in one hand and a much-used palette in another. He looks haggard, his body ravaged by time. His neck and face are so thickly layered with paint that, through patches of black, blue, purple, and brown, they did not seem to represent the human flesh at all.

Yet when she stepped back to look at the painting, she could see not only how real the body seemed, but also how the paint resembled the actual flesh of an old man, with wrinkled skin and softening muscles. She read in the catalogue what the painter thought about his work: 'I want paint to work as flesh . . . As far as I'm concerned the paint is the person.' It was disconcerting, for here was someone who was essentially saying: 'The person does not matter; the work is everything.'

But the person does matter, and it matters more when one loves. It is a precarious way to live, when one loves another as a body in time, in the flesh, for it means it has to be this body, this particular lived life, while the person is still in the world. It is a faith built on the most fragile of foundations, yet isn't its very fragility making it valuable and true?

6

AT ROSE'S FIRST MILONGA a few months ago, she was invited to dance by a dashing stranger, a grey-haired man in a double-breasted dove-grey suit.

She told him she was fairly new to the dance while they waited for the music to start; she said that she really needed his guidance. She was in the beginning of envisioning a new dance in her mind: a tango danced *en pointe* for the woman, with the man maintaining the fluid movements of the traditional tango. She had only danced the tango a few times before, and she loved the style of 'close embrace,' with the woman's upper body leaning on the man's for support, a slow dance full of unacknowledged tension and release. But she wanted to push the female dancer to do more than extending the lush lines of her legs; she wanted the sublime grace of her dancing on *pointe* shoes, soaring above the pull of gravity.

Upon hearing this, the grey-haired gentleman quietly removed her left hand from his right shoulder, and pressed her palm flatly on his chest, right in the middle of his ribcage. Then he asked very courteously, almost apologizing, whether he could place his right hand on her chest as well. She nodded without quite knowing what she was consenting to, and felt his hand gently pressing her between her ribs, just above her breasts. Then he stood close to her to get ready for the dance, their arms bent, his cheek touching her forehead, his free hand falling by his side.

They were now connected by their hands on each other's chest, and there was almost a reverence in the way he touched her. She suddenly felt a little light-headed when they leaned towards each other like this, waiting for the musicians to start. It was not because of their incredible physical intimacy, which was something she was accustomed to as a dancer, but because of the way he regarded her. He was treating her as a woman, not a dancer, and his courtesy was the courtesy of a suitor.

'Please keep your torso as close to mine as possible, and you should also push me away with your hand as much as you can,' he whispered in clear, accented English. Those were the last words they exchanged; everything else happened wordlessly.

When the music finally began, a song of exquisite melancholy, played by a trio of violin, bandoneon, and double bass, he started walking slowly towards her, forcing her to walk backwards, staying close to him yet pushing him away, each step balanced by the union of their heads and torsos, and by their bent arms that kept them apart. Each movement of their legs became part of these long, luxurious sequences of advance and retreat; she felt almost intoxicated by the tension that made the dance possible.

Later, Emma, who took her to the milonga, told her that she and the Argentine looked like they both knew what they were doing, that they seemed very much in control of their steps. But Rose knew she had learned much more than how to dance the tango. She had learned to dance deliberately through the force of tensions that she used to think were untenable. She had started to learn to dance as if she were in love.

7

'HAS THIS ALREADY happened to you?' She wants to ask him. Something deepens in her today. In the few short months she has known him, the desire he had aroused in her dazzled her, dazed her, made her light-headed, short of breath, on the verge of fainting. Like that song her mother loved, 'Lilac Wine,' sung by Nina Simone, which she used to hear as a child coming from her mother's room late at night: 'Lilac wine is sweet and heady, like my love. Lilac wine, I feel unsteady, like my love.'

But tonight when she thinks of him, picturing him having an early dinner by himself in a little café somewhere, something new slowly settles within her, not in her chest, but in her belly, in that most vulnerable,

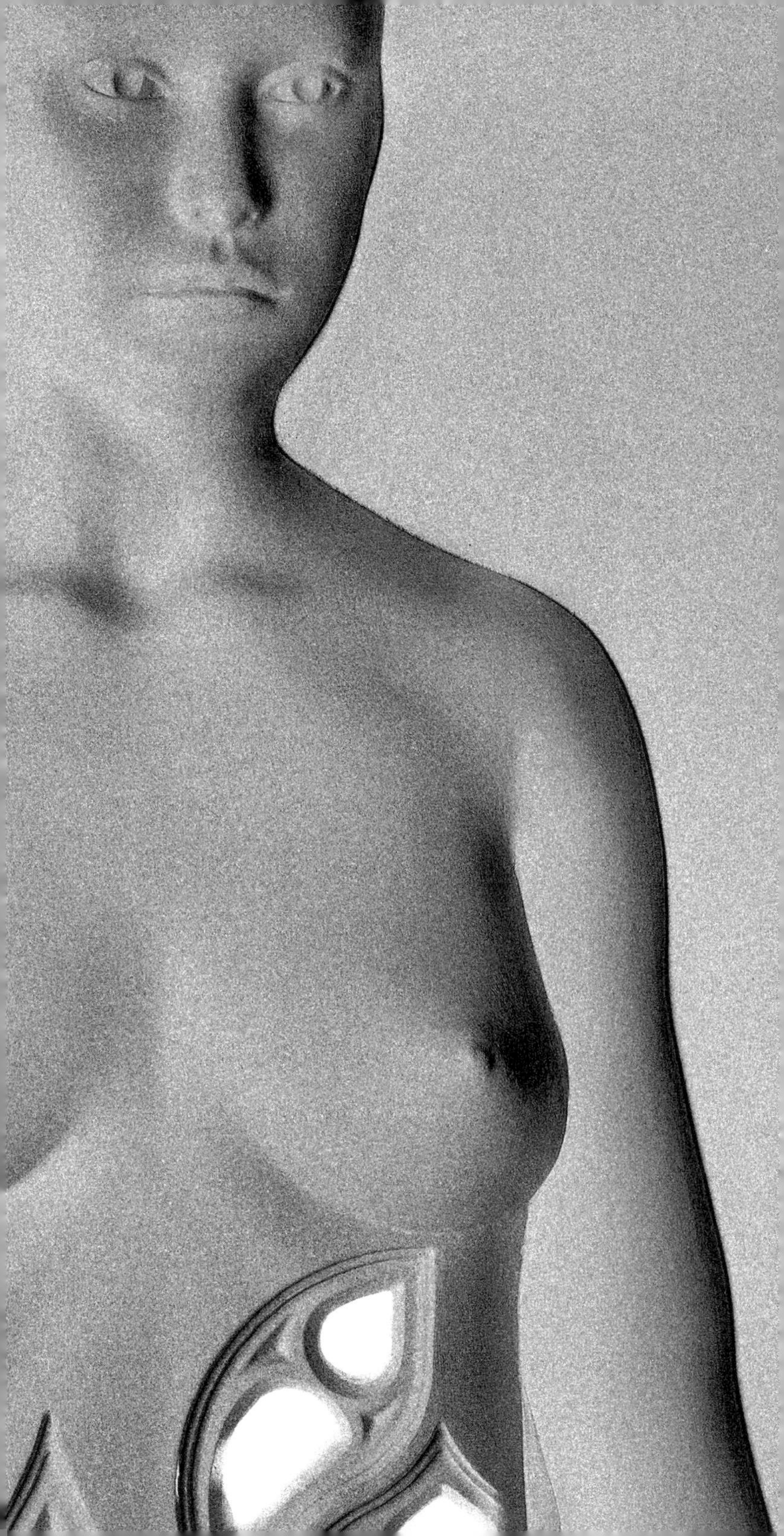

fragile space between the ribcage and pelvis, that part of the body where one's sense of the self secretly resides, the source of one's deepest and truest voices, movements, and desires. And she feels him falling and disappearing into her, into that warm, dark place, and she knows that she has taken him into her being. It is going to hurt if she were to let go of him.

8

THERE WAS A MOMENT two weeks ago, in her dance studio, when she took David's photos out of a large envelope, and laid them on the floor. They were taken by a professional photographer to be used alongside an interview in the university paper. The last time Rose saw David, she told him she liked the photos, and asked if she could have copies. He said that it seemed too egotistical to impose his pictures on her, but she insisted. The photos arrived from the photographer's studio only a week before spring break, after he had been missing for almost two months from her life.

The photos were large prints of black and white, showing him standing next to a sculpture on campus, or sitting in an armchair in his office. She has to make up her mind about whether to use him – his spirit, his presence, the sensations he evokes – for the developing of her dance. She could imagine him being her tango partner, and she could come up with movements that would be true of his character, his temperament, his physical attributes. It was not merely an imaginary exercise; once he became part of the dance, she would no longer see him as the complex person that he was, the real person that he was. He would cease to be actual to her, and become a part of her work process, a means to the creation of a work of art. She has done this before with others; she knows that once a person becomes the source material for art, the choice is irreversible, with the work always taking precedence over the real.

That day in her studio, she caressed the photos that were scattered on the floor. There was his hair, his forehead, his eyes, his mouth, his hands. Should she stay true to what had transpired between them? What if he is a sensualist of the heart, and it is only the experience of seduction that he is after? But he had already disappeared from her life, so suddenly and without explanation; she could no longer allow her heart to be consumed by such uncertainty, anxiety, doubt.

9

WAITING IN HER ROOM for the next prayer to start, a scene from a Russian novel she read a long time ago, at the urging of her father, comes to Rose's mind.

In delirious moments of love, Dr Zhivago imagines that he is opening up his beloved Lara's right shoulder with the tip of a sword, like turning a key in a hidden lock. Now her body yields the deepest secrets of her life: streets of faraway cities that she has lived in; faces of people she has loved; experiences she has treasured. They are now all unfolding right before his eyes like a roll of ribbons, as if in an ancient myth.

Rose could let go of David now to preserve her own sense of safety and composure, and he will disappear from her life, never to be seen in this way by her again.

His journey through the next stages of his life will be unknown to her; she will not be there to comfort him, or to be comforted. If she lets him go now, she realizes, she cannot ever speak of her love for him, for it is not love, but merely weightless desire. She would remain a sensualist of the heart herself, after all.

And yet – and yet – 'what is actual is actual only for one time.'

10

SHE REALIZES, with astonishment, that she has never truly loved before. She has cried while making love, moved by the ephemeral feelings of deep connection with the person in her arms, their bodies seeking a communion when everything else in their lives seems false and inconsequential.

But she now sees that she has in fact been a connoisseur of mere emotional pleasure. She is familiar with the subtle indications of attraction, delicate acts of seduction, and she has allowed herself to become someone who savours the intense moments of yearning as if they were well-aged wines, listening to the vibrations of her own heart as if it were an instrument of enjoyment. She has allowed herself to take on emotional involvements simply because they bring her strong sensations of delight or longing, yet she has steadfastly resisted giving herself to anyone, not even the ones she claimed to love.

How flawed they both are, she thinks: she with her intense emotional indulgences, he with his relentless distrust of passion and love. Perhaps they have connected not because of their love for each other, but their love for themselves. And perhaps that is how they recognize each other: two ships passing each other in the dark ocean when most others have already safely anchored in the harbour, a sheltered life that seems forever beyond their reach.

11

IF SHE WERE TO LOVE AGAIN, she says to herself in the empty church after Vespers, she needs to love differently. Her love cannot be about herself, but about the person she loves; her love for David has to be about what he needs, not what she desires.

As she sits alone on the balcony, she notices for the first time a small tree near the high altar, the sole decorative item in this high-ceilinged white space. The tree is still young, with thin branches supporting large green leaves, and the beautifully defined shape of the leaf – almost heart-like – looks uncannily familiar.

Then she suddenly remembers: this is the Indian Bodhi Tree. Legend has it that the Buddha reached enlightenment while sitting underneath the Bodhi Tree, struggling with the demon Mara and his entourage; thereafter it became the most sacred plant in Asia. She knows about it because her father had a small Bodhi Tree in his study, grown from seeds a student of his brought back from India, and he would do his daily meditation on a cushion next to it. He would also pick up the fallen leaves and save them in old editions of classical Chinese poetry. In fact, he once gave her a volume that had at least a dozen heart-shaped leaves in it. She remembers feeling annoyed by his obsession over a tree, especially when he seemed to care so little about his only daughter's life.

How unexpected yet how strangely fitting it is to see her father's sacred tree growing in this monastic sanctuary, here on a silent spring evening.

She lets out a deep breath, letting go of her past anger and hurt. And she tries to learn, for the first time, to love without desiring anything in return.

12

ROSE GOES TO COMPLINE in a daze. There is an openness to her heart that seems to be changing the way she sees the world.

After the prayers, the young woman from Texas taps Rose on the shoulder, signalling that it's time to go downstairs for the nightly blessing from the Abbot. This is something Rose has been doing in the past few nights. The Abbot gives his benediction to the monks after Compline, so they may enter the darkness of the night with his blessings. The retreatants are welcomed to the benediction after the monks are blessed.

The Abbot stands in the middle of the church, facing people who are walking in two lines towards him. With a slight lifting of his hand, he spreads drops of water onto their faces from a silver container with a freshly cut pine branch.

There is purposeful silence throughout the benediction: no music, no chanting. The only sounds in the Abbey church are people's footsteps, and occasionally birds can be heard through an accidentally opened door.

13

SHE WALKS TOWARDS THE ABBOT with her head lowered. The tense conversation she had with the Abbot yesterday is now coming back to her vividly, and she is conscious of how she might appear to the head of the monastery as someone who is unworthy of his blessings.

When she is finally standing in front of the Abbot, she makes herself look up, dreading a look of disapproval from him. But he is smiling warmly at her, a smile not dissimilar from what she has seen on her brother's face, when he still loved her, when he was still part of her life.

DAY SEVEN

The Fire and the Rose

SHE WAKES VERY EARLY in the morning, and the clock on her phone says it's not yet three. She turns up the brightness of the lamp on her night-stand, even though its fluorescent rays are too harsh for her eyes. She sits up in bed, forcing herself to stay awake.

She did not sleep well at all. She vaguely remembers the fragmented dreams from her unsettled sleep in which Leo treated her as if she were a total stranger. In her dream she was merely mystified by it, but now the hurt slowly awakens, a numbing pain in her chest that would not go away.

She gets out of bed, walks barefoot to the small bathroom, and splashes cold water onto her face. Her cheeks look pale in the mirror, her lips bloodless. She no longer remembers why she is here, or what she is looking for in this cold, stony place. She is no longer needed by Leo; in this empty, strange room, she is more alone than ever, and she is left facing all her fears and anxieties without even the small comforts of home. The consolation of familiar music or books is not within her reach; there is nothing that can distract her from facing the expanding void. The ground is no longer solid under her feet; the sea is coming in before the sun rises.

She turns off the lights, walks over to the window, and draws open the grey curtains that cover the long, narrow glass. It is still pitch black outside. She sits down in the chair by the window and tries to pray.

SHE DOES NOT SAY A PRAYER, yet somehow she knows that she is praying, for she is finally giving herself completely to the darkness, something she has long feared. It is as if she were at last wading into the shallow water of the innermost shore of the sea.

She has nothing to hold onto anymore, nor anything to lose; she is finally surrendering herself to the night, to the sea of the unknowing, no longer trying to stay on safe ground, no longer fighting for reassurance and certainty. Deep in her heart she is ready for the drowning: if she loses her sense of self and goes under the dark waves, so be it. Now she has reached a place in her life in which a free fall is better than living forever in fear.

She does not know how long she will be sitting here. She tries to keep her body still, her mind clear, waiting for something to happen to her, something that will release her from this darkness that seems to permeate all her senses. At one point she hears the bells for Vigils, but she lets them go without moving from where she is sitting. She simply waits patiently in the dark.

It is not as difficult as she imagined to stay still for so long. Her dancer's body keeps her back straight in the hard chair, but gradually her back relaxes, her spine following the chair's gentle curve. Her hands simply rest on top of each other in her lap. Her heartbeat grows quieter after some time; she can no longer hear the exaggerated sound of blood rushing through the veins in her ears, a sign of true calmness for her.

An hour passes, then another. She hears the bells for the next prayer, Lauds. It is almost six in the morning.

And although the sky is still dark, she can begin to make out the heavy contours of the trees outside the window, ink-black shades against the dark-blue of the sky.

3

THEN, SUDDENLY, before she could comprehend it, the first ray of daylight breaks through the dark space before her. There is a barely visible glow shining from within the darkness, a brightness falling from the air. It is as gentle as a whisper, yet it quietly pierces her heart.

Although she does not move, her body responds to it by taking in an involuntary deep breath, as if she were finally surfacing from the bottom of the sea, now gasping for air. Within minutes the soft light saturates the dark space, casting a luminous clarity onto everything around her. Suddenly she can see clearly the dewy green leaves outside her window, the white walls around the Abbey. The world is being reborn right before her eyes, saved from the eternal shadows of the night. Before she realizes, it is already a bright morning under a cloudless spring sky.

Sitting by the window, she has the completely unexpected feeling of being freed from something heavy in her heart. The anxieties and fears that have been clinging to her are falling away in this tender light, as if they were rocks falling into the deep bottom of the ocean, freeing her from their unbearable weight.

She feels herself unfolding like a kite, opening herself up to the sky and the wind. She feels that the radiant, silvery morning light is about to carry her away.

4

SO IT IS WORTH IT, after all. It is worth it to surrender, even with all her doubts and unhappiness, for it brings her closer to this moment of clarity, when the purest meanings of her life are revealed wordlessly, bestowed to her like grace.

5

FATHER BERNARD SEES ROSE sitting in the dining room after breakfast, a cup of coffee held in both hands, waiting for the next prayer, Terce, to start.

He sits down in front of her, and she tries to smile to him, but tears well up in her eyes instead. He pats her hand, and says gently: 'What do you do after having been here? What will you do with your life?'

6

SHE REMEMBERS READING somewhere that Kierkegaard thinks of monks as navigation buoys at sea. They mark the frontier of human endurance, devotion, and faith. They also mark the edge of how far we can venture into the dark unknown. They show us, through their hard-earned life experience, the strength and limit of humanity.

Rose knows that she does not have the rigour to be there herself. But she has seen, even only through a distance, even only for a few days, the ones who are out there in the deep end of the ocean, day after day, night after night. They are both guarding and leading her, and she now knows how much she needs their strength in order to carry on.

7

HOW SHE MISSES the Abbey already, even before leaving it . . .

She stands in the middle of the empty dining room in the retreat house, looking out at the bright morning sky. Her body already knows and remembers when it is time for Vigils, for Terce, for Compline, and she aches to follow each divine office once again.

8

ON THAT TRIP TO BIG SUR, Leo had asked Rose whether she thought it was possible to lead an absolute life. Certainly not, Rose said. Following the absolute would only result in disappointments and disillusionments. What if one suddenly realizes God does not exist, after years of devotion? What if love fails, after one loves unconditionally?

Perhaps there is nothing beyond human faith, Rose now sees with a clarity that surprises herself. What makes belief real is seeing these monks who lead devoted lives every single day, starting before dawn. And love – what makes love real is the absolute fidelity and purity of one's heart.

How she does not want to turn David into merely a means to some insignificant end, using him for an exquisite experience of love without actually loving him. How she wants to do justice to him through her love, even at the risk of her own jeopardy, in time and in the real world. Love is costly, yet love is the only salvation too.

The complete surrender of the self. The total giving of the self. Is she ready for it in her own life? Will she ever be ready for it?

9

ROSE WALKS UP TO THE BALCONY of the Abbey church for Sext, her last divine office here. She has to leave soon after the prayers, not even staying for lunch, for she has a long drive back to New Jersey.

The Abbot starts the prayers after a few minutes of meditation, as usual, and signals the beginning of the office by lightly hitting a wooden block on the wooden stall, a sound she has now grown to love.

There is prolonged silence after the last prayer, chanted slowly, with an almost imperceptible gentleness:

> Lord, have mercy.
> Christ, have mercy.
> Lord, have mercy.

Then the sound of the wooden block breaks the stillness, and everyone on the balcony stands until the last monk leaves.

There is total silence in the white Abbey church while the monks walk back to the monastic enclosure, following their abbot in a single file. The austere ceiling is as high as a cathedral's, now filled with brilliant sunshine.

10

ROSE SAYS A SILENT GOODBYE to her brother as she watches him walk away, the last person in the slow moving line of monks.

Leo's long arms are again folded behind him, a gesture she remembers from their childhood, which now sends a gentle tremor through her heart. He does not lift up his eyes to look for her on the balcony; his eyes have not met hers even once during her week here. Yet she now understands that he still loves her, that he loves her more than ever.

11

THE DAY IS STILL GETTING WARMER as she prepares for her departure, with heat rising from the growing crops around the Abbey, the dark soil of the open farmland, and the brightness of the midday sun.

She has left a letter for Leo with Brother Thomas in the guest-house. Nestled in a white envelope are two small pages:

My dearest Leo,

I have seen you, and now I have to go back to the world. I don't know if I can ever manage to explain your action to others – something I've always failed to do in the past! But after spending a week here, after seeing you in prayer, I think I'm beginning to understand your new life. The question is: How should I change my life after seeing what you have done?

I know you probably think you've already said goodbye to me when we went to Big Sur last year, even though I didn't know it at the time. But you won't be able to leave me behind; I will always be your sister, and I will always think of you when I read a book you might love, hear a song that you might like, make a meal the way you make it, or see something beautiful or true – how much I will miss the deep and intense way you respond to the world. You might think that you are finally alone here, without family or friends, without any emotional attachment, so you can devote yourself to God, so you can live a pure, absolute life. But you are still loved – I will love you always, even if we may not see or speak to each other again, even if you no longer need such human, transient interactions.

And when you pray in your white church at three in the morning, remember that someone who loves you is asleep somewhere in the world, one of those numerous, tiny stars outside the windows in that great darkness, and that your prayers are what protect her from fear and despair.

I will come back to see you, Leo. I love you always,

Rose

12

SHE STANDS IN THE SUN in the garden, watching two monks working on the lawn near the end of the garden. She has just phoned David to tell him that she is going to meet with him tomorrow night in New York, at the opera.

He didn't say much. He simply responded: 'I will have a bottle of champagne ready at home.' There was palpable joy in his voice, but there was a quiet tremor too, as if he unexpectedly lost his bearing when he heard her voice. It sounded as if he were suddenly becoming vulnerable, unsteady, in danger of falling. She could hear her own firm heartbeat carrying her forward, so she could be strong for herself as well as for him.

The day is perfect: the sky blue and cloudless, the open fields smooth and green, the air infused with the strong scent of grass and unknown flowers. This is a spring day that should be remembered. There are a few children running around in the fields on the other side of the road, far away from the monastic estate, but she can still hear their laughter, carried over by the light wind.

13

SHE SAYS HER FAREWELL to the Abbey, and says a prayer.

She feels something opening up in her like a flower in the sun. Her hard shell of caution, reserve, and self-protection slowly falls away; her trust in something beyond herself grows with each word of her simple prayer. She feels the centre of her being unfurl petal by petal, layer by layer, and something deep in her heart finally opens, something infinitely gentle, fragile, and true.

She has not felt so vulnerable in her life. And she has never felt safer, more protected, more loved.

14

MY LOVE, she says silently, I am no longer afraid.

Trappist, Kentucky and Paris